"You just can't he you?"

She struggled to keep her voice level. "You have to embarrass me."

"Mi dispiace," he purred, his eyes glinting wickedly. "I'm sorry—unfair of me, I know. It's just that I love watching you blush. Your cheeks are the same color they will be after we've had frantic sex."

"That is never going to happen. Accept it."

"That shows how little you know me. I have a compulsive need to change situations that aren't to my liking." He smiled—a slow, dangerous smile. "It's called negotiation."

"Negotiation is when both parties get what they want—it's supposed to be a win-win situation."

"I understand the winning bit. I'm not so good at accepting half a solution." His tone was gently apologetic, but his dark eyes were as cool and unemotional as ever. "When I want something, I want all of it. Not part of it."

"You're not my type, Alessio."

"That's what makes it so exciting, *tesoro*...."

Dear Reader,

Harlequin Presents® is all about passion, power, seduction, oodles of wealth and abundant glamour. This is the series of the rich and the superrich. Private jets, luxury cars and international settings that range from the wildly exotic to the bright lights of the big city! We want to whisk you away to the far corners of the globe and allow you to escape and indulge in a unique world of unforgettable men and passionate romances. There is only one Harlequin Presents®, available all month long. And we promise you the world....

As if this weren't enough, there's more! More of what you love. Two weeks after the Presents® titles hit the shelves, four Presents® Extra titles join them! Presents® Extra is selected especially for you—your favorite authors and much-loved themes have been handpicked to create exclusive collections for your reading pleasure. Now there's another excuse to indulge! Midmonth, there's always a new collection to treasure—you won't want to miss out.

Harlequin Presents®—still the original and the best!

Best wishes,

The Editors

Sarah Morgan

CAPELLI'S CAPTIVE VIRGIN

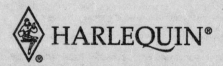

HARLEQUIN®

TORONTO • NEW YORK • LONDON
AMSTERDAM • PARIS • SYDNEY • HAMBURG
STOCKHOLM • ATHENS • TOKYO • MILAN • MADRID
PRAGUE • WARSAW • BUDAPEST • AUCKLAND

Recycling programs
for this product may
not exist in your area.

ISBN-13: 978-0-373-12829-7

CAPELLI'S CAPTIVE VIRGIN

First North American Publication 2009.

Copyright © 2009 by Sarah Morgan.

All rights reserved. Except for use in any review, the reproduction or
utilization of this work in whole or in part in any form by any electronic,
mechanical or other means, now known or hereafter invented, including
xerography, photocopying and recording, or in any information storage
or retrieval system, is forbidden without the written permission of the
publisher, Harlequin Enterprises Limited, 225 Duncan Mill Road,
Don Mills, Ontario, Canada M3B 3K9.

This is a work of fiction. Names, characters, places and incidents are
either the product of the author's imagination or are used fictitiously,
and any resemblance to actual persons, living or dead, business
establishments, events or locales is entirely coincidental.

This edition published by arrangement with Harlequin Books S.A.

® and TM are trademarks of the publisher. Trademarks indicated with
® are registered in the United States Patent and Trademark Office, the
Canadian Trade Marks Office and in other countries.

www.eHarlequin.com

Printed in U.S.A.

All about the author...
Sarah Morgan

SARAH MORGAN was born in Wiltshire, U.K., and started writing at the age of eight, when she produced an autobiography of her hamster.

At the age of eighteen she traveled to London to train as a nurse in one of London's top teaching hospitals, and she describes those years as extremely happy and definitely censored!

She worked in a number of areas after she qualified, but her favorite was the Accident & Emergency department, where she found the work stimulating and fun. Nowhere else in the hospital environment did she encounter such good teamwork between doctors and nurses.

By now her interests had moved on from hamsters to men, and she started writing romance fiction.

Her first completed manuscript, written after the birth of her first child, was rejected by Harlequin®, but the comments were encouraging, so she tried again. On the third attempt her manuscript *Worth the Risk* was accepted unchanged. She describes receiving the acceptance letter as one of the best moments of her life, after meeting her husband and having her two children.

Sarah still works part-time in a health-related industry and spends the rest of the time with her family, trying to squeeze in writing whenever she can. She is an enthusiastic skier and walker, and loves outdoor life.

to think clearly. She hadn't slept for three nights, the panic

CHAPTER ONE

'SIGNOR CAPELLI doesn't have an opening in his diary for five months.' The stunning blonde receptionist spoke faultless English and was clearly experienced in providing an impenetrable shield between her sexy billionaire boss and the public. 'You wouldn't believe the demand for divorce lawyers of his calibre. And anyway, his personal clients are all men.'

Lindsay dug her nails into her palms. 'I don't need a divorce lawyer. That isn't why I want to see him.'

And she *knew* his clients were men.

She knew everything about him. She knew that when a man instructed Alessio Capelli to handle his divorce, the wife in question might as well give up. The ruthless Sicilian lawyer had apparently made it his life's mission to ensure that women gained as little as possible from the end of a relationship. She also knew that his various business interests had made him a billionaire in his early thirties, which meant that he now worked purely for entertainment value.

And what sort of man found entertainment in crushing people's fragile marriages?

The girl tapped a perfectly manicured nail on the glass desk. 'I could call one of his team?'

'I need to speak to *him*.' Eaten up by worry, Lindsay tried to think clearly. She hadn't slept for three nights, the adrenaline was surging round her body and she felt physically sick as she contemplated what was unfolding before her. 'Please— I've flown to Rome specially—it's a personal matter. Something between myself and Signor Capelli.' A vision of her sister's pale face tormented her, but Lindsay had no intention of revealing her family secrets to this glacial beauty.

It was an unnerving experience—trying to gain access to the last man in the world she wanted to see. A bit like stepping towards the edge of a very sheer, crumbling cliff face, knowing that there could be only one outcome.

She was going to fall—

The receptionist raised her beautifully shaped eyebrows and it was obvious from her disbelieving gaze that she found it unlikely that someone like Lindsay would ever share anything personal with Alessio Capelli. 'Did he give you his mobile number?'

'No, but—'

'Then clearly he doesn't want you to contact him. Women who have a *special* relationship—' the receptionist paused for emphasis and gave a faintly patronising smile '—always have that number.'

Lindsay wanted to tell her that her taste in men didn't run to arrogant, heartless marriage wreckers, but she sensed that she wouldn't be believed.

Alessio Capelli was a magnet for women. His profession should have acted as a deterrent but instead it seemed to increase his appeal—as if every woman on the planet wanted to prove that they could win over this notorious cynic.

She stepped aside as another beautiful girl sauntered up to the bold curve of glass that formed the ultra-modern reception desk. 'The boss is in the gym, taking out his frustrations on a punchbag. If that file he is waiting for ever arrives, send it straight up to him on the sixteenth floor.'

As she listened in to the conversation Lindsay's gaze slid towards the bank of elevators at the back of the foyer. *Could* she? Her heart skipped a beat at the shear audacity of the idea. No, she couldn't possibly. She didn't break rules—

But somehow her feet were walking—quickly.

Waiting to feel a hand on her shoulder at any moment, Lindsay shot through the open doors and slammed her shaking hand onto the button that said sixteen.

As the doors closed she felt nothing but relief and then realised that her respite was only temporary.

She still had to get to Alessio Capelli.

Her heart was pumping, her palms were clammy and she fumbled with the lock of her bag as she searched frantically through the work she'd brought to do on the plane. *Work she'd been too worried to touch.* Exactly what sort of file was Alessio Capelli waiting for? Something buff-coloured and formal? Thick? Thin? Something in a sealed envelope? Hands shaking, she pulled out a file and tucked it under her arm. It didn't look particularly official, but it would have to do.

Sick with nerves, she checked her appearance in the mirrored wall. Looking back at her was a serious young woman dressed in a crisp white shirt and a straight black skirt that stopped just above the knee. Her pale blonde hair was twisted into a severe knot at the back of her head and her make-up was discreet and professional. She looked—businesslike.

No wonder the receptionist hadn't thought she was the sort of woman likely to have attracted the attention of Alessio Capelli, a man renowned for being seen with *extremely* beautiful women.

Something stirred inside her. A tiny spark of female vanity that she tried almost instantly to suppress.

But she *had* attracted his attention, hadn't she?

Once.

Once, he'd noticed her. In fact he'd more than noticed her. If she hadn't rejected him, they'd have—

Lindsay put her hands on her skirt and slid it slowly up her thighs until it revealed the same amount of leg as the girl downstairs had been showing. She stared at herself for a moment. Then she gave a nervous start and let the skirt drop just as the lift doors opened.

For crying out loud—*what was she thinking?*

Trying to look confident, she approached a set of glass doors manned by a muscular security guard.

Alessio Capelli certainly made sure he was well protected, she thought dryly, wondering whether it was because of his indecent wealth or the number of enemies he'd made in the pursuit of that wealth.

He was hard, cynical and ruthlessly ambitious. Unfortunately he was also sexier than any man had a right to be and Lindsay felt a moment of pure panic as the moment of confrontation grew closer.

She focused her mind on her sister.

Ruby. This was about Ruby, not her.

Ruby was her one and only priority.

'I'm here to see Alessio Capelli.' She smiled at the security guard. *'Sto cercando il Signor Capelli.'*

The man looked at the file under her arm and immediately punched a number into a keypad. The doors opened, revealing a state-of-the-art gym offering an incredible view over the rooftops of Rome.

Despite the breathtaking architecture, it was an all-male domain—the atmosphere thickened by testosterone, the room a melting pot of male ego, pumped muscle and raw aggression.

The security guard took one look at her uncertain expression and gestured towards a man who was throwing hard, rhythmic punches at a bag.

'That's him. That's the boss.'

Lindsay was grateful for his help because, without it, she never would have been able to identify the infamous Sicilian.

It wasn't what she'd expected of a billionaire with a taste for the finer things in life. But perhaps it was symbolic, she thought wryly, that Alessio Capelli had chosen this particular method of keeping his body in top physical condition. Did he run or lift weights like the other men in the room? No. He chose to thump the living daylights out of something.

Which simply confirmed what she already knew—that he was a tough, ruthless, cold-hearted machine who knew nothing about emotion.

Several of the other men glanced in her direction and suddenly she felt as vulnerable as a lone gazelle finding itself in the middle of a pride of lions.

Gritting her teeth, Lindsay kept her own eyes forward and followed the security guard across the room.

Alessio Capelli hadn't seen her. He continued to pound his fists into the bag, the muscles of his arms and shoulders bunched in a display of physical force. His bronzed skin gleamed with sweat and his shorts and vest top displayed a physique honed to perfection by hard, punishing exercise. His shoulders were wide and powerful, his body athletic as he threw punch after punch with ruthless precision and impeccable timing.

Watching this display of brutal male aggression, Lindsay faltered, sure that the security guard had made a mistake.

This was the wrong man. It wasn't him.

It was six months since she'd seen him, but Alessio Capelli's smooth sophistication and startling good looks were still inconveniently lodged in her brain. Not that it had been looks alone that had drawn her attention. For her, the quality that had made him dangerously attractive was his astonishing intellect. He was a man who used his razor-sharp brain to twist legal precedent to his advantage. His weapon was words, and he used them with lethal skill to achieve the outcome he wanted, whether it was winning a case or seducing a woman into his bed. As a lawyer he was, she knew, the very best.

As a human being—

Lindsay flinched as the man in front of her punched his fist hard into the bag. There was nothing smooth or suave about this particular man. On the contrary, he seemed to represent masculinity at its most basic level.

And then the angle of his body shifted and Lindsay drew in a sharp breath because she could now see the tiny scar above his left eye and the slight bump on his nose that blemished an otherwise faultlessly handsome face.

Once seen, never forgotten.

Every inch of his cold, hard features was etched into her memory for ever.

Horrified by the sudden flash of awareness that exploded through her body, Lindsay took a step backwards regretting the circumstances that had forced her into his path again.

Averting her eyes from his spectacular body, she suddenly wished he were dressed in a formal suit and standing on the other side of a very large desk.

How could she possibly have a serious conversation here?

He was half naked, for goodness' sake.

Half naked and *angry*, if the power behind those rhythmic punches was anything to go by.

That missing file had obviously been something important.

He still hadn't noticed her and it crossed her mind that she could still slink away and wait outside the door for him to finish his workout.

And then his gaze shifted and he stilled.

Dark, deep-set eyes connected with hers and in that single moment the world seemed to shrink. Nothing existed outside the square metre that contained the both of them.

They stared at each other in silence, exchanging a long, lingering glance that was wholly sexual. Trapped by the intimate demands of his intense dark gaze, Lindsey felt the blood pound in her head and she ceased to breathe.

He'd had exactly the same effect on her the first time she'd seen him and it was as terrifying now as it had been then.

Even knowing who he was and what he did for a living had done nothing to lessen the sheer physical impact of the man. He was unashamedly and blatantly masculine, his Sicilian roots evident in every bold line and hard angle of his impossibly handsome face. Stripped virtually naked, he was even more breathtaking. Unlike most men, he had no need of clothes as a disguise for physical imperfections. Alessio Capelli looked even better undressed than he did dressed.

His eyes were dark and framed by such thick, long lashes that it was as if nature had decided to emphasise such an unusually striking feature with extra care. Other men might have used those lashes as an effective screen for his emotions, but not Alessio Capelli. His gaze was direct and unflinching and she suspected that the reason he never felt the need to conceal his emotions was because he'd never actually experienced an emotion of any sort in his life.

He dealt with facts and numbers. And they were *big* numbers if the rumours were correct.

Feeling eighteen rather than twenty-eight, Lindsay cleared her throat. 'Hello, Alessio.'

His fists dropped to his sides and his eyes didn't leave hers. Then he slowly removed each of his gloves and dropped them onto a nearby bench.

'You've chosen a romantic venue for a reunion, Lindsay.' He spoke in perfect English, but in every way that mattered he was pure Sicilian. The dark good looks, the arrogance, the simmering volatility barely held in check by the veneer of sophistication that surrounded him like another skin—all products of his ancestry.

A wicked thrill of pleasure that he hadn't forgotten her was immediately replaced by dismay.

Flouting the powerful messages from her brain about not responding to him, her insides tumbled with excitement and her knees weakened. *This* was why she didn't trust herself around him—every second that she was in his company, her life became a battlefield. She was instantly trapped in a vicious conflict between what her body wanted and what her brain wanted.

The layers of protection she'd built around herself melted away in an explosive blast of raw chemistry. Her grip on the present slipped, and her mind twisted the highly charged sexual attraction into the ugly, destructive monster she knew it to be.

Terrified by the sudden glimpse into her own vulnerability, Lindsay reminded herself again that this was about Ruby. *Ruby was the reason she was here.*

'I'm surprised you haven't forgotten me, given the number of blonde women in your life. They must merge after a while.'

Amusement shimmered in his eyes as he reached for a towel. 'The unexpected is always memorable. You walked away from me.'

And she could tell from his tone that no woman had done that before.

'There was never the slightest possibility that I'd become involved with you. Unlike you, I think with my head.'

He laughed at that, and Lindsay frowned slightly because over the months she'd managed to forget that he had a sense of humour. And she knew why—that sense of humour made him seen more human and she didn't want to think of him in that way. It suddenly seemed vitally important to remember that he was cold, ruthless and unemotional. In her head he needed to be as unattractive as possible.

But the smile he gave her was anything but unattractive. 'So why are you standing in front of me now?'

'I'm here because I need to talk to you.' And that was true. But it didn't change the fact that she was painfully aware of him. *And he knew it.*

Alessio Capelli had so much experience with women that it would have been impossible for him *not* to know and the slow lift of his brow confirmed it.

'You have flown all the way from England just to talk to me? I didn't realise you found my conversation so stimulating.'

Lindsay was trying hard to ignore his superior height and the width and power of his shoulders. She hadn't needed a display of his boxing prowess to be aware of his strength. Strength was woven through his very being; an essential part of the man. Everyone who came up against him crumbled. Physically and mentally he was a titan.

And he made his living from using that strength against others.

Against women.

Suddenly she wished desperately that she could wind the clock back. If she could have done so, then she wouldn't have chosen Rome for a city break and she definitely would have paid more attention to where she was walking late at night.

Indirectly this whole situation was her fault.

If she'd never met him he would have remained in her head as a professional adversary instead of a man. When their paths had crossed professionally she would have been wearing her protective cloak, instead of which—

'I tried calling you from England,' she said crisply, 'but no one would put me through to you. I've travelled here purely because you're *impossible* to get hold of. Your staff will never say where you are. How do your clients contact you?'

He wiped his hands on the towel. 'If you were a client,' he said evenly, 'you would have been given a different number to call.'

The same number as his women? Dismissing that thought,

Lindsay bit her lip. 'I told them on the phone that I wanted to talk to you about a personal matter—'

'Then it's hardly surprising that they didn't put you through. They know that I never discuss personal matters.'

'I said it was urgent.'

'Which they would have translated as meaning that you were a journalist working to a tight deadline.' He looped the towel around his neck and Lindsay frowned slightly, wondering what it was like to lead the sort of life where everyone wanted to know everything about you.

'That was why no one would answer my questions? Because they thought I was a journalist?'

'I've trained my staff to be suspicious. A tiresome necessity driven by being in the public eye.' A cynical smile on his face, he stooped to retrieve a bottle of water from the floor. 'I'm intrigued as to what could possibly be important enough to drag you back into my disreputable presence. Hopefully you've finally decided to abandon those principles of yours and explore the endless pleasures of emotionless sex.'

'Alessio—'

'You've no idea how much I'm looking forward to getting you naked, *tesoro*.' His dark drawl connected straight to her nerve endings and she felt a flash of heat low in her pelvis.

He was doing it on purpose, she knew he was. *Trying to unsettle her.*

'You just can't help yourself, can you?' She struggled to keep her voice level. 'You have to embarrass me.'

'*Mi dispiace,*' he purred, his eyes glinting wickedly. 'I'm sorry—unfair of me, I know. It's just that I just love watching you blush. Your cheeks are the same colour they will be after we've had frantic sex.'

'That is never going to happen. Accept it.'

'That shows how little you know me. I have a compulsive

need to change situations that aren't to my liking.' He smiled—a slow, dangerous smile. 'It's called negotiation.'

'Negotiation is when both parties get what they want—it's supposed to be a win-win situation.'

'I understand the winning bit—I'm not so good at accepting half a solution.' His tone was gently apologetic but his dark eyes were as cool and unemotional as ever. 'When I want something, I want all of it. Not part of it.'

Her heart was racing out of control and her thoughts were going in much the same direction. 'You're not my type, Alessio.'

'That's what makes it so exciting, *tesoro*.' He was clearly enjoying teasing her, tying her in knots. 'If your taste in men ran to dangerous divorce lawyers, it would be boring. The chemistry between us must be very inconvenient for you.'

The conversation had taken a dangerous direction.

It's like sailing a ship through a storm, she thought wildly. *Almost impossible to keep it from being blown off course.*

He took her somewhere she didn't want to go.

Somewhere she'd marked as off-limits a very, very long time ago.

'Ruby—' she croaked. 'I'm worried about Ruby.'

'Ah.' His eyes narrowed slightly. 'I should have known that your sudden arrival would have something to do with the disappearance of that racy, naughty little sister of yours.'

'Disappearance? So you don't know where she is, either?' His words successfully dampened the sexual chemistry that had been threatening to eat her alive. Deeply troubled by that piece of unwelcome news, Lindsay sank her teeth into her lower lip, her mind speeding ahead, sifting through the options. 'I thought—I hoped that you'd know what was going on. I thought she might have said something to you.'

'Why would she do that?'

'Because you're her boss! She's been working for you for the last six months.'

'And you think I spend my working day exchanging confidences with my administrative staff?' Alessio lifted the water bottle to his lips and drank deeply and Lindsay watched in dazed, mesmerised silence, momentarily distracted by the bronzed column of his throat and the tangle of dark, male chest hair at the curve of his vest. Intercepting her gaze, he lowered the bottle slowly and a hint of a smile touched his hard, sensuous mouth. 'It's unwise to look at me like that,' he warned silkily, 'if you don't intend to follow through. And we both know that this isn't the time or the place.'

The knowledge that he'd read her so easily was almost as disturbing as the unexpected and unwelcome burst of warmth that erupted low in her pelvis. 'Do you ever think of anything other than sex, Alessio?'

'Yes.' Relaxed and in control, he scanned her flushed cheeks with disturbing intensity. 'Sometimes I think about money.'

Lindsay looked away briefly, furious with herself for giving him the opportunity to increase her discomfort. 'Can we *please* just talk about Ruby?'

'If we must.' His tone shifted from bite to boredom and he glanced at the clock on the wall. 'Obviously you're still trying to exert your authority over her.'

'It isn't about authority. I love her and I care about her.'

'As long as she is living her life the way you think she should live it. I don't claim to be an expert on love, Lindsay, but I think it's something to do with accepting people as they are and not trying to change them. You grip her like an eagle holding its prey.'

Lindsay felt a stab of pain, hurt by his criticism of her relationship with Ruby. He had no idea. *No idea what their lives had been like.* The quicksand of her emotions shifted and she stayed still, not allowing herself to be sucked down by the past. 'As you say, you know nothing about love.' *She wasn't going to let her mind drift backwards.* 'She hasn't phoned me for a week and that's not like her. She isn't answering her phone and when I called your office they said that she hasn't been in but they don't seem to know any more than that. I'm worried. Really worried.'

'Worried that she's slipped out of your grasp? She's twenty-one. Old enough to make her own mistakes without any outside interference.' He adjusted the towel. 'And it appears that she's done just that.'

Lindsay stood still, tortured by a moment of self doubt. *Was* she interfering? No, this was her sister they were talking about. 'Ruby is extremely vulnerable. When we met you and your brother last summer—well, she'd just come out of a very destructive relationship. She was devastated and—' She broke off, reluctant to reveal anything about their past. 'On the surface she seems all bubbly and together but— You may think you know her, but you don't.'

His eyes fastened on her face. 'She's been working for me for the past six months. I suspect that I know a great deal more about your sister than you do.' His tone was dry. 'And now you'll have to excuse me. I'm seeing a client in an hour and I'm flying to the Caribbean after that. Which is where, incidentally, your sister should be. She was supposed to be assisting me with a big case.' He strolled through a pair of swing doors and Lindsay hesitated briefly before following him.

Client—case—

He was obsessed with work; totally focused on generating still more wealth to add to his billions. Why?

Frowning slightly, Lindsay dismissed the question instantly. She wasn't interested in what had turned Alessio Capelli into a ruthless, money-making machine. All she cared about was her sister. And he'd just revealed a small amount of information. Not much—just a morsel, but at least it was something.

'She knew you were expecting her to go to the Caribbean?'

'Of course. She was in charge of all the logistics both before and during the trip.'

'There's no way Ruby would have just abandoned her responsibilities like that—' Lindsay stopped dead, realising that she'd followed him into the changing room.

Fortunately for her it was empty, but Alessio threw her a challenging glance, a sardonic gleam in his dangerous dark eyes. 'You intend to continue this conversation while I shower?' He pulled the tee shirt over his head, his lack of concern about his semi-naked state in direct contrast to her own growing discomfort.

Faced with a full-on display of breathtaking male physique, Lindsay felt her heart thud hard against her chest. 'Could you just—not do that for a moment—?' Her voice cracked and she tried again. 'All I'm asking for is a few minutes of your time to talk. Please.'

'If all you want is to talk, then the going rate for a minute of my time is about a thousand dollars. Unless you've suddenly won the lottery, you couldn't possibly afford me. However, if you *don't* want to talk then I'll consider a preferential rate.' His gaze raking her flushed cheeks, he gave an unsympathetic laugh. 'What's the matter? If you're shocked, then you have only yourself to blame, *tesoro*. If you follow a man into the shower then you need to accept the consequences. It probably isn't the best action for someone who is trying to deny the sexual side of their nature.'

'I'm not denying anything. Yes, there's chemistry between us—' incurably honest, she stumbled over the words '—but that doesn't mean I have to act on it. Being an adult is about taking responsibility for your choices.' His amused glance set fire to her cheeks and Lindsay lifted her chin. 'You're *not* my choice.'

'No?'

Somehow the conversation had become personal again and Lindsay lifted a hand and rubbed her fingers over her forehead. This wasn't how she'd planned it. She'd been determined not to make it personal. 'Please—can we just talk about Ruby?'

'Of course. You talk. I'll shower. If you're so confident about your "choices", it won't bother you to see me naked.' His hands dropped purposely to his shorts and she inhaled sharply and averted her eyes.

He was trying to unnerve her, she knew that, and the best response would have been to stare boldly at him and say something cutting, but her brain had turned to treacle and her tongue wouldn't move.

'Outside,' she muttered incoherently. 'Perhaps I should wait for you outside—'

'Why would you need to do that?' His voice was silky soft. 'Not having problems with your "choices", are you? Not finding that famous willpower of yours tested? Is that why you're wearing the formal suit and the prim hairstyle? You're hoping that if you're tightly buttoned up on the outside, the inside will follow?'

'I came straight from work.'

'Ah, yes—your work. Lindsay Lockheart, relationship counsellor. How's that all going? The last time we were interviewed by the same radio show you were earnestly urging people to use RAP, your new Relationship Analysis Programme.' He sounded amused. 'I tried it out with my last girlfriend. Unfortunately I finished with her before we reached the end of it.'

Lindsay bit her lip. 'You don't need my programme to identify that your relationships are all shallow and meaningless. The programme isn't designed to factor in the emotional shortcomings of a cynic like you.'

'So perhaps you should release a version called the Cynic's Relationship Analysis Programme.' He smiled. 'Conveniently shortened to CRAP.'

Her face burned. 'I'm not here to rehash our professional differences.'

'I've always been intrigued as to how you've managed to build a reputation as an expert on relationships when your own experience in that area is so limited.'

It was as if he'd stripped off her clothes with the slice of a knife and left her vulnerable and exposed in front of him. Lindsay suppressed a helpless shiver, trying to find the weapons to fight him.

But confrontation wasn't her speciality.

No wonder he was unbeatable as a lawyer—he identified a person's weakness and then he pounced without hesitation or conscience.

If it weren't for Ruby she would have been out the door and back on the plane.

As it was she forced herself to focus on Ruby again.

'I need to know if my sister is involved with your brother.' *Please say no*, she begged silently. *Please say that isn't what's happened here.* 'She was definitely seeing someone, but she was very cagey about it and that isn't like her. Normally she tells me everything.'

'Everything? So that you can enjoy a vicarious sex life?'

Lindsay gritted her teeth. 'Could they be together? Could she be having an affair with Dino?'

'I'm sure she could. They seemed to find each other—entertaining.'

A cold trickle of dread ran through Lindsay's veins. 'And you didn't try to stop them?' Even without looking she was conscious that he'd removed the rest of his clothes and she kept her eyes firmly fixed on the wall. 'It didn't occur to you that they're *totally* unsuited?'

'Unlike you, I don't make it my business to interfere. My control streak doesn't extend to managing other people's relationships. And I am not my brother's keeper.' Arrogantly confident, he strolled towards the showers and she caught a glimpse of hard male muscle, strong thighs and bronzed skin. Then he closed the door and she heard the sudden rush of water.

Momentarily released from his presence, Lindsay sucked in a breath and blinked back tears of frustration and worry. If circumstances had been different she would have walked away because when it came to verbal sparring she was no match for him. He tied her in knots. But his words had left her deeply worried for her sister and frustrated by his lack of support.

As far as she was concerned, this was the worst-case scenario. It appeared that Ruby *was* involved with his brother, to the extent that she no longer even cared about her job.

If Alessio was telling the truth, then her sister had abandoned her responsibilities.

What would have made her do that?

Why would she have behaved in such a reckless, irresponsible fashion?

And why hadn't Alessio put a stop to it when it was obvious that the whole thing was going to crash and burn in the most disastrous way possible?

Couldn't he see? *Couldn't he see that a relationship between Ruby and Dino was an accident waiting to happen?*

Lindsay stared angrily at the shower cubicle.

Yes, of course he could see that. But he didn't care about anyone but himself.

He had no idea what that sort of relationship would do to Ruby.

It crossed her mind to tell him the whole tragic story in the hope that it might appeal to his sense of decency. But she honestly didn't think Alessio Capelli had a decent side.

What had possessed her to come here?

It had been a completely wasted journey.

They were so, so different in their approach to life, their beliefs—everything.

Feeling another rush of concern for her sister, Lindsay tried to think as she might. Where would Ruby have gone? What exactly had she done? *And why had she done it?* 'Did you encourage them?' She raised her voice to be heard above the shower and the sound of water stopped suddenly.

He emerged from the shower, a towel looped around his lean hips, his mouth curved into a cynical smile. 'Even you can't be *that* naïve. Two hormonal adults don't need encouragement, Lindsay. All they need is opportunity.'

'And I've no doubt you created that opportunity.' Rubbing her forehead with the tips of her fingers, Lindsay tried to think clearly. 'You encouraged them, I know you did. You knew how strongly I felt about the two of them becoming involved. When we first met, I told you Ruby was just getting over a broken relationship. She was—incredibly vulnerable. Still is. Your brother is the last thing she needs at the moment.' Lindsay swallowed. 'Did you do this on purpose? To punish me because I refused you? Was this about your ego, Alessio?'

Dark lashes veiled his gaze. 'If you're looking for somewhere to lay blame for your sister's behaviour, perhaps you should look a little closer to home.' His tone several shades cooler, he gave a careless shrug. 'If anyone is to blame for the way your sister lives her life, then it's surely you.'

'Me?' Genuinely shocked by that harsh analysis, Lindsay gaped at him. 'That's ridiculous. I've always warned her against having meaningless affairs and I certainly warned her to stay clear of you and your brother.'

'Precisely. For a relationship counsellor, you clearly know very little about human nature.'

'What's that supposed to mean?'

'That the forbidden and the dangerous is always more exciting than the permitted and the safe,' he said flatly. 'I can guarantee that the day you warned her to stay clear of me was the same day she showed up at my office looking for a job.'

'And you gave her one.' She couldn't keep the reproach out of her voice and he gave a dismissive shrug.

'There was a vacancy in my administrative team. Ruby is decorative, sociable and a relatively competent secretary.'

'Relatively?'

Alessio's mouth curved into a faint smile. 'Well, she's not here, is she? She does have a tendency to become—easily distracted.'

'By your playboy brother, presumably.' Frustration mingled with anxiety and Lindsay shook her head. 'You didn't think that throwing the two of them together might not be a good idea?'

'I allow *my* sibling to lead his own life. And unlike you I don't see anything wrong with animal passion. On the contrary, I endorse animal passion. It's one of the few truly honest human emotions.' With a casual movement Alessio unhooked the towel and threw it carelessly over the nearest bench. 'You ought to try it some time.'

Blinded by a disturbing vision of raw masculine perfection, Lindsay felt her mouth dry and looked away quickly. 'You're doing this on purpose,' she muttered hoarsely, 'trying to unnerve me.'

'Does it unnerve you my being naked?' As relaxed as she was tense, he ripped the packaging from a fresh shirt and thrust his arms into the sleeves. 'That's interesting. Next time you're analysing behaviour, you might want to dwell on that. Deep down, buried underneath that layer of control, is a real woman trying to get out.'

'Ruby.' Her voice hoarse, Lindsay kept her eyes fixed on a point on the wall, trying to erase the shockingly vivid image of dark body hair and substantial manhood. 'We were talking about Ruby. You don't even care that she might have gone off with your brother.'

'On the contrary, I do care. I'm as keen as you are to contact her. You can look. I'm decent.'

'You are? I mean—you want to know where she is, too?' Relief flooded through her. Perhaps she'd misjudged him. He did, after all, have a human side. 'Then what have you done so far? Have you tried to contact your brother?'

He'd pulled on a pair of beautifully cut dark grey trousers, but the white shirt still hung loose, affording a tantalising glimpse of masculine chest hair shading hard muscle. 'Like your sister, he isn't answering his phone. I suspect they're otherwise occupied.'

Lindsay made a distressed sound. 'But *you* can find them. I know you have contacts. It won't take you long to track them down.'

The snowy-white silk shirt seemed to emphasise his masculinity and Alessio threw an amused look in her direction as he fastened the buttons with slow, deliberate movements of his long fingers. 'Your belief in the degree of my influence is quite sweet. Do powerful men turn you on, Lindsay?'

'Please stop it.' A hoarse whisper was all she could manage because her body was in such a turbulent state. 'Please, please stop it. I'm just relieved that you're as keen as I am to intervene before this relationship goes too far.'

'I have no intention of intervening in the relationship.'

Confused, Lindsay frowned. 'But you said—'

'I said that I am as keen as you are to find out where Ruby is—' he reached for his silk tie '—but *not* because I intend to counsel her on her choice of men. I believe in letting people make their own mistakes in life.'

Lindsay just stared at him. 'Then why are you keen to find her?'

'Under the terms of her contract, your sister was obliged to give notice if she intended to terminate her employment. She hasn't.' With skilful grace his fingers produced a perfect knot and he eased the tie up to his bronzed throat. 'If she doesn't turn up for work by four o'clock this afternoon, she loses her job. I thought it only fair to warn her of that fact.'

There was a buzzing in Lindsay's ears. 'You're going to *fire* her?' The words came out as an appalled squeak. 'That's ridiculous.'

'That's business. I employed her to do a job. She's not doing it. Be grateful I'm not suing her for breach of contract.' His tone hardened and she gazed at him in shock.

'Even you can't be that hard-hearted.'

His eyes held hers. 'What would you say if I went back to my office this afternoon and fired someone on the spot?'

'I'd say you were a megalomaniac,' Lindsay said faintly and a smile flickered at the corners of his mouth.

'You'd say I was unfair. Employers and employees have a certain responsibility towards each other. I'm a fair employer but I expect the same degree of fairness in my employees. I expect a certain code of behaviour. Your sister broke that code. I intend to make an example of her.'

Lindsay closed her eyes. If she'd thought things were bad before this conversation, they were fast becoming worse.

'No.' She shook her head in disbelief. '*Please* don't do this—Ruby really likes working for you.' *Although she'd never understood why.* 'Losing her job would be devastating.'

'It will send a clear message to other employees to think twice before they wilfully abandon their contracts.' Showing not a glimmer of remorse or uncertainty, he reached for his jacket. 'Your sister has until four o'clock. If she isn't on my plane, ready to do the job for which she is employed, then her time with my company is over.'

'Alessio, I'm begging you not to do this—'

His gaze lingered on her face. 'Normally I have no problems with a woman begging, but on this occasion you're wasting your time. If she isn't here within the hour, she's fired.'

CHAPTER TWO

LINDSAY stood in stunned silence, wondering how a bad situation had suddenly become so much worse.

Ruby was about to lose *everything*. 'Please don't take her job away from her. When her relationship with your brother crashes, Ruby is going to be devastated.'

'Only if she has unrealistic expectations about relationships, which, being your sister, she undoubtedly will have.'

Reminding herself that an argument on that topic would get her nowhere, Lindsay bit her lip. 'If she loses her job as well, it will finish her.'

'Or perhaps it will teach her an important lesson about loyalties, priorities and the fact that actions have consequences.' His tone was unsympathetic. 'Ruby is employed by me to do a job. If she can't or won't do it, then I don't want her on my team.'

'She's a junior member of your secretarial staff. I'm sure you have literally *hundreds* of people who could easily take her place on this trip of yours.'

'That isn't the point. This is Ruby's responsibility. If she lets me down, she's out.'

'If she lets you down then you should fire your brother!' Lindsay glared at him. 'He's as much to blame for this situation as Ruby. More because he's eight years older than her!'

'My brother runs his own area of the business—his actions are of no interest to me.' Displaying not a whit of sympathy, he slipped his Rolex onto his wrist and fastened it. 'Stop trying to run her life. You can't protect her from everything. This might be just the wake-up call that Ruby needs. I'm sure it will prove to be a useful life experience for her. There's nothing quite like a few knocks to toughen a person up.'

What did someone like him know about knocks? He went through life giving them, not receiving them. Someone with his wealth and confidence knew *nothing* about struggling to survive. *Nothing about uncertainty and insecurity.*

'Ruby *needs* this job. And she's usually very responsible. This isn't like her. I don't understand it.'

'My brother and Ruby couldn't keep their hands off each other. It's called passion,' he said dryly. 'It happens to the best of us.'

'But they didn't have to act on it. They're not children,' Lindsay said tartly. 'They should have known better.'

His gaze dropped to her mouth and lingered there with disturbing intensity. 'You've never been so overwhelmed by passion that you throw caution to the wind?'

Her face burned scarlet. 'I'm an adult, Alessio, not a teenager. And one of the characteristics of adulthood is the ability to exercise self-control when the need arises.'

For some reason he seemed to find that amusing. 'That comment makes me wonder whether that legendary self-control of yours has ever been truly tested.' His gaze lifted to hers, his dark eyes burning with sexual challenge. 'When did you last struggle not to rip a man's clothes off, Lindsay?'

When she'd first met him—

Before she knew who he was and what he did for a living.

Her heart was bumping against her chest. 'We were talking about Ruby.'

He smiled. 'So we were. Well, your sister is either lacking

your iron self-control, or she is a master tactician who has her eye on a higher prize. There's always the possibility that she's hoping that my brother will marry her.'

'Ruby isn't interested in marriage.'

'All women are interested in marriage if the prize is high enough.' His tone was deeply cynical and Lindsay shook her head.

'Ruby knows that your brother isn't the marrying kind any more than you are.' But he'd scattered doubt in her mind. *Did* her sister know that? Or was she deluding herself, as so many women did once they were in the throes of passion? 'We both know that their affair isn't going to last five minutes.'

Alessio raised his eyebrows. 'They did your CRAP test?'

Lindsay flushed. 'We both know that they're not in love. Theirs is a relationship based on casual sex. To be successful, a relationship has to be founded on real intimacy. But that's something I don't for a moment expect you to understand.'

He gave a slow smile. 'I don't have any problems with intimacy, Lindsay. In fact, intimacy is my favourite method of relaxation.'

Her entire body warmed under his lazy scrutiny and she straightened her shoulders, instinctively rejecting her response. 'I'm talking about *emotional* intimacy.'

He leaned his wide shoulders against the wall, a wicked sparkle in his eyes. 'By emotional intimacy I assume you mean a cuddle after sex.' Tilting his glossy dark head to one side, he pretended to consider the point for a moment. 'I'm not totally averse to that, providing the woman in question has pleased me. I can be generous when it suits me.'

She knew he was winding her up and she also knew that she was getting herself deeper and deeper into trouble. The atmosphere was suddenly impossibly tense and she told herself that it was just because they were talking about sex.

'Let's just not even discuss this,' she muttered faintly. 'You and I will *never* agree on what makes a good relationship.'

Under the penetrating force of his dark gaze she felt heat rush through her body.

'A good relationship is one that ends when it is time for it to end,' he said dryly, 'and doesn't struggle along for years in mortal agony.'

'Oh, please.' Determined to ignore everything that was happening to her, Lindsay made an impatient sound. 'Next you'll be telling me that divorce lawyers do the human race a favour.'

'Not the whole human race. Just a select few who I believe to be worthy of my particular skill set.'

'You make money out of people's misery.'

'So do you,' he returned instantly, the glint in his eyes suddenly hard. 'The difference between us is that I've built a successful business based on reality, whereas yours is based on fantasy. You peddle dreams. Fairy tales. Happy ever afters.'

'That isn't true—'

'Expecting a relationship to last in today's society is the stuff of fantasy.'

'That isn't true either—'

'Then why is my phone always ringing? Why am I busier than I've ever been?' Cool and calculating, he watched her. 'Because people are finally accepting that expecting to be hooked to someone for life is totally unrealistic. Better to do what my brother and your sister are currently doing—have wild exciting sex until it is no longer exciting. Then move on.'

Listening to him rip holes in everything she believed in, Lindsay felt her limbs tremble. 'I *completely* disagree with you.'

His eyes lingered on her mouth. 'Well, of course you do. If you didn't, you'd be out of a job. I watched you on television last week, recommending ways in which a certain Hollywood actress could save her marriage. Lindsay Lockheart, relationship expert. You look cute on the screen, by the way.' His voice was dangerously soft. 'Cute and convincing, which is all the more surprising when you bear in mind that Lindsay Lockheart, relationship expert, has never actually had a relationship herself.'

Ignoring the mockery in his eyes, Lindsay defended herself. 'It's true that I've never been married, if that's what you mean.' Her heart pumped hard because he was pressing in close to a subject she avoided.

He studied her in silence, his expression thoughtful. 'It wasn't what I meant. Do your clients know that you're a fraud, Lindsay?' His tone pleasant, he slipped his arms into his jacket and her face flamed.

'I've had relationships, Alessio.'

'I'm not talking about a dinner date or a dignified trip to the opera.' With unconscious grace, he strolled purposefully towards her, suddenly looking every inch the sophisticated, successful lawyer. Gone was the street-fighter image of moments earlier. The transformation from rough and tough to slick and sophisticated was complete. Dressed in a dark grey suit that moulded his powerful shoulders to perfection, he exuded wealth and success. The only thing that hadn't changed was the air of raw power that clung to him like a second skin.

Lindsay felt her heart rate double and fought the impulse to take a step backwards. No way was she going to let him have the upper hand. He'd stop in a moment—he had to.

But he didn't.

He strolled right up to her and backed her against the wall, decisive, masculine and very much the one in control.

Flustered, she lifted her hands and then dropped them again. 'Alessio, for goodness' sake—'

'I'm not talking about a staid exchange of views over a quiet drink in one of your English country pubs. I'm talking about an explosion of passion, real intimacy.' He planted a powerful arm on either side of her head, blocking her escape route. 'I'm talking about *real* intimacy, Lindsay. Hot, sticky, exciting intimacy—intimacy that makes your heart race and makes you forget that you have responsibilities—'

'Alessio—'

'Intimacy that's out of your control. Intimacy that drives you to bad decisions. I'm talking about man-woman stuff.' His eyes glittered, dark and dangerous, and his mouth was suddenly terrifyingly close to hers. 'Animal instinct.'

'Alessio!'

'Ever felt that, Lindsay—' his breath was warm against her mouth '—the sort where logic and self-control don't get a look-in?'

He was going to kiss her.

This time, Alessio Capelli was going to kiss her.

There was a buzzing in her ears, her knees felt like jelly and her stomach burned with wicked sexual excitement. Even as her brain struggled to resist it, she could feel herself going under, submerged by swirling waters of dark, danger-ous passion.

The damaged child inside her was screaming at him to go away, but the woman inside her wanted him right where he was.

His gaze held hers for a long moment and then his arms dropped to his sides and he took a step backwards. '*That's* the sort of relationship I'm talking about, little Lindsay.'

Her heart was pounding so hard that for a moment she was terrified that she might actually pass out. She blinked several times to clear her vision and forced herself to breathe slowly. And then humiliation rushed through her veins because she knew she'd been microseconds away from sliding her arms round his strong neck and pressing her mouth against his. 'I don't know what you're talking about.' It wasn't disappointment she was feeling. It absolutely wasn't going to be disappointment.

'I know you don't. And that's the point I'm making. How

the hell has someone like you managed to carve out a career for yourself advising couples on their relationships?'

It wasn't safe to be this close to him. And not because of him.

She just couldn't trust herself— 'Just because I haven't made a mistake—'

'Your idea of a mistake is another person's idea of a life,' he said dryly and she clasped her hands in front of her.

'You're talking about meaningless sex—'

'And you don't think two people can have a relationship based on meaningless sex?' His eyes narrowed. 'Trust me, *tesoro*. A relationship based on meaningless sex is the best sort.'

His remark restored her common sense. 'Which brings us right back to the point I made earlier—' strength ran through her veins and she met his gaze bravely '—that you don't know anything about true intimacy. Intimacy is not a cuddle at the end of sex. Intimacy is about sharing. Real love is about sharing thoughts and feelings, hope and fears.'

Alessio gave a faint smile. 'Then I'm truly relieved that I've managed to avoid your type of "intimacy",' he drawled. 'And people's spurious belief in something they call love is what keeps my phone ringing.'

Lindsay gave an exasperated sigh. 'Love exists. And if you've never experienced that first-hand or witnessed it, then I feel sorry for you. It must be very cold and lonely in your bed.' She regretted the words instantly and, sure enough, his sensual mouth curved into a wicked smile.

'Generating heat in my bed isn't one of my problems,' he drawled softly, 'so any time you need a practical demonstration of alternative energy sources, just bang on my bedroom door, *tesoro*.'

Lindsay lifted her fingers to her forehead and breathed deeply. 'I suppose it's your job that's made you so very cynical—'

'Realistic,' he slotted in helpfully. 'It's made me realistic. Which is why I haven't had to pay out a fortune in alimony.'

'You have no experience whatsoever of sustaining a loving, intimate and accepting relationship.'

His gaze was mocking. 'Of course "loving, intimate and accepting relationship" can be conveniently shorted to LIAR, a word which effectively describes everyone who claims to be happily married.' He glanced at his watch. 'Fascinating and absorbing though this discussion is, I have an anxious client waiting in my office, eager to eradicate the last LIAR in his life, and I'm due to fly to the Caribbean immediately after that.'

Flustered, she tried to marshal her thoughts. 'But Ruby—'

'Console yourself that Ruby is, at this moment, probably having the best sex of her life. If she happens to have the sense to show up at the airport, I'll suggest that she calls you,' he said in a cool tone. 'If not, then next time you do speak to her, you can advise her to start looking for a new job.'

Emotionally shattered by her encounter with Alessio, Lindsay sat alone in the café, her tiny cup of espresso coffee untouched on the table in front of her.

It had been worse than she'd feared. *So much worse than she'd feared.*

Despite all her efforts, just being near the man unsettled her and it had become harder and harder to think of Ruby.

Even now, as she tried to focus on her sister's plight, her mind was haunted by Alessio Capelli's dark, sardonic smile.

Lindsay stared blankly at the dark, pungent coffee in the tiny cup, wishing for the millionth time that her sister had never taken the job.

For Ruby—young, impressionable and so desperately wounded after her last disastrous relationship—the lure of a job in sun-baked Italy, in the employment of a sophisticated billionaire, had proved too tempting to turn down.

A fresh start, she'd called it.

More like 'out of the frying pan into the fire', Lindsay

thought wearily, remembering just how hard she'd tried to persuade Ruby to see sense.

'Alessio is a typical Sicilian male. He might seem very modern and charming, but underneath—' she tried hard to make Ruby see the truth '—underneath he's ruthless, macho and his view of women is firmly stuck in the Stone Age.'

Dark eyes staring into hers, demanding her attention.

'You didn't think he was so unbearable when he saved our necks that night by the Coliseum. If he and his brother hadn't happened to be passing—' Ruby gave an expressive shudder. 'They were amazing. I mean it was like something out of a movie, wasn't it? The two of them taking on that gang of thugs and they beat them easily.'

Lindsay just looked at her sister helplessly, not knowing what to say.

It was all too easy to see how Ruby might have been seduced by the romance of the whole situation, because for a short time she'd felt the same way.

Once Alessio Capelli had dispensed with the gang who had surrounded them, he'd lifted her gently but decisively to her feet, his sexy dark eyes faintly quizzical as he'd studied her in the dim light.

For that one breathlessly exciting moment, she'd forgotten who, and where, she was.

With his broad shoulders and superior height, he'd seemed so powerful and *safe* that she'd actually swayed towards him, driven by the delicious and unfamiliar curl of desire low in her pelvis.

Looking back on it now, she realised that she probably would have been safer with the gang that had attacked them.

Fortunately for her, Alessio had released her before she could make a complete and utter fool of herself, but not before he'd awakened a part of Lindsay that she'd previously refused to recognise.

The two brothers had taken them to the bar of the most expensive hotel in Rome, a venue so exclusive that Lindsay wouldn't have had the courage to put her toe inside the door of such a place if she hadn't been with them.

Overawed by the opulent surroundings, it had been several minutes before she'd noticed the deference of everyone around her and several more minutes to realise that the arrogant, powerful man currently extending a glass of champagne in her direction actually *owned* the hotel. Vastly entertained by the fact that she had no idea who he was, he'd introduced himself properly and it was at that point that everything had fallen apart for her.

Alessio Capelli.

Of all the men who could have come to her rescue, it had been Alessio Capelli, the ruthless divorce lawyer who had a reputation for protecting his male clients from 'gold-digging' women.

The irony was, she knew him. Their paths had crossed professionally. They'd never met in person, but they'd been interviewed on several occasions by reporters keen to publicise their opposing views on relationships. And as she'd familiarised herself with his opinions, Lindsay had gritted her teeth and fumed. When asked to comment on some of her techniques for predicting marital success he'd been scathing and derogatory in his remarks.

And as if that weren't enough, she'd worked with some of his clients on an individual basis. She'd seen first-hand some of the damage he'd wrought.

'Alessio Capelli crushes women,' she told her sister flatly, but Ruby simply shrugged.

'Not all women. Just the greedy ones. You didn't think he was so objectionable when he used his muscle to save you from that lowlife. I bet he's a *fantastic* kisser.' Ruby gave her a wicked look. 'Rumour has it that what Alessio Capelli doesn't know about seducing women isn't worth knowing.

Come on, Linny. I know you always use logic and common sense, but you have to admit he's *gorgeous*. And if you don't like your men dark and intimidating, there's always his cute younger brother…'

Lindsay clamped her lips together, deciding not to point out that only two weeks earlier Ruby had been so devastated over the end of a relationship that she hadn't seen the point of living.

'Ruby—try and be a bit more analytical,' she urged. 'Think beyond the handsome face. Do you have the same views on life? Do you share the same values? Do you have what it takes to sustain a relationship?'

'I'm just having fun, Linny. Not planning a wedding,' Ruby snapped at her. 'You're *so* serious. You should have an affair with Alessio Capelli. It would do you good. A week of sun, sex and hot Sicilian man.'

Closely followed by a lifetime of heartache.

'I'm not interested in a meaningless affair with someone whose values I don't respect. And we're talking about you, not me. I just don't think you should get involved with anyone else for a while,' Lindsay said tactfully and Ruby's eyes clouded slightly.

'Don't worry. I've learned that lesson.'

Lindsay stared at her cold coffee now.

Had she?

Or was Ruby in the middle of yet another wild, crazy affair that would undoubtedly lead to another major emotional crash?

Her thoughts driving her almost demented with worry, Lindsay reached for her phone and called everyone she knew one more time. But still no one had any news of Ruby.

So now what?

Feeling helpless, she glanced at the clock on the wall of the café. Ruby had less than an hour to make the flight.

She tried to think positively.

There was still time for Ruby to turn up. She knew the importance of reliability in the employment market—she wouldn't let Alessio Capelli down…

Suddenly Lindsay felt an ominous stabbing pain above her eye and winced as she recognised the beginnings of a migraine. *Oh, no, not now.* And not here, in a foreign country where nothing was familiar.

Gritting her teeth, she reached into her bag for the packet of tablets she carried with her. But there was no sign of them. With a frown, she emptied the contents of her handbag over the table and rummaged through it. No tablets.

Infuriated with herself for forgetting to replenish the tablets last time she'd used them, Lindsay swept the items back into her handbag and tried to think clearly. Normally she'd take a tablet, lie down for a few hours and emerge revived.

This time she had no tablets and the hands of the clock were relentlessly moving towards four o'clock. She didn't have time for a headache. She knew what Ruby was capable of doing—

Drenched with sudden panic, Lindsay forced herself to breathe slowly—to *think*.

What could she do?

With something approaching desperation, Lindsay pressed her fingers against her temples, searching for alternative options.

The knifelike pain in her head increased and she closed her eyes. But with her eyes closed she had a sudden vision of Ruby's pale lifeless face and she shot to her feet in the grip of an overwhelming panic. It took a moment to wrestle her overactive imagination back under control and remind herself that she had no evidence that anything bad had happened to Ruby.

There was probably a perfectly simple explanation for all this.

Perhaps her phone was broken, or perhaps she'd simply lost track of the time and had every intention of returning to the Capelli offices in time for the Caribbean trip.

Perhaps she was there now, offering an apology for her lateness to Alessio Capelli.

Keeping that thought uppermost in her mind, Lindsay reached for her bag and paid for her coffee.

Perhaps, she thought as she left the café, this whole nightmare would have a swift and happy ending.

CHAPTER THREE

ALESSIO CAPELLI rode the glass elevator down to the ground floor of his office building, ignoring the insistent buzz of the telephone that was tucked in the pocket of his suit.

He should have been rejoicing. In one short meeting he'd gained another high-profile, influential client and, more to the point, he'd ripped him away from a rival law firm. Ruthlessly competitive, Alessio waited for the usual high that came from defeating an adversary, but this time there was nothing.

Instead his brain was dominated by a picture of a pair of troubled blue eyes and blonde hair so tightly secured at the base of her slender neck that not even a strand was likely to escape.

Control, he thought dryly. Lindsay Lockheart was big on control. She controlled her hair, she controlled her emotions, but most especially she controlled her little sister.

For a woman who made her living trying to modify human behaviour, Lindsay was appallingly naïve when it came to understanding the actions of her younger sibling.

He'd never met anyone so serious. She acted as though she were ninety, and yet he knew she was only in her late twenties.

He strode across the polished marble floor of the lobby, through the revolving glass door and out into the street where his car awaited.

As if conjured straight from his thoughts, there was

Lindsay Lockheart. She was standing by his car wearing the same crisp white shirt and slim black skirt that she'd had on earlier, her small overnight bag clutched in her fingers. Her delicate chin was held at a certain angle and there was a hopeful look in her eyes that melted into anxiety as she saw that he was on his own.

His driver shot him a look of nervous apology and Alessio sighed, lifted a brow in sardonic appraisal and focused his gaze on her pale face. 'If you want to spend more time conversing, then I'm going to have to bill you.'

She stepped towards him. 'Has Ruby turned up?'

'You are obsessed with your sister's movements.' He handed his case to his driver, noting the way her cheeks blanched. It was a strange sibling relationship, he mused. Just how far was Lindsay prepared to go for her wayward sister? And, more interestingly, why?

'I love my sister,' she said huskily, 'and I won't apologise for that. Nor do I intend to explain myself to you.'

'A decision that leaves me quite weak with relief,' Alessio confessed in a lazy drawl, his eyes drawn to the tempting thrust of her breasts through her perfect white shirt. 'I can't imagine anything more likely to challenge my attention span than a summary of your family history. So, if you haven't come to bore me, why are you here?'

'I was checking whether you'd heard anything. I thought she might have turned up to do her job.'

'Sadly for Ruby, the answer is no.'

Her slim shoulders sagged slightly as he delivered what was clearly a very unwelcome piece of news. 'Could you give her a few more minutes? Just in case?'

'No,' he said gently, 'I couldn't.'

She closed her eyes briefly and he saw that her lashes were long and thick, the skin on her eyelids as pale as the rest of her face. 'Please—' Her voice cracked and when she opened her eyes again there was desperation there. 'I—I know we don't agree on things, but this is really important to me. Is there anything I can do to stop you firing her?'

The wild and wicked side of him took over. 'Come in her place.'

He made the demand in absolute confidence that she would refuse.

The way they lived their lives was diametrically opposed.

On the surface they clashed, conflicted and disagreed.

But perhaps the biggest discordance lay *under* the surface. The powerful pull of sexual attraction disturbed her and he had a strong feeling that the roots of that disturbance were to be found deeper than the obvious restrictions posed by her ridiculously idealistic belief system.

He knew there was no way that Lindsay would ever voluntarily put herself in his path, so when she responded with a shocked 'I can't do that,' he shrugged, reflecting on the fact that being constantly right could border on the tedious.

'Of course you can't.' He couldn't resist goading her a little more. 'To be trapped with me in a romantic Caribbean hideaway would be a completely unfair test of your willpower. I understand.'

'You flatter yourself, Signor Capelli.' Her voice shook and her cheeks had slightly more colour than they had a moment earlier. 'I could lie naked in a bed with you and still have no trouble resisting you because I know you're just not right for me.'

Alessio laughed, thoroughly enjoying himself. 'Now *that's* a challenge no red-blooded Sicilian could refuse.'

'I wasn't issuing a challenge,' she said stiffly. 'I was merely pointing out that the brain does actually play a prominent part in my decisions although I can understand that you, as a "red-blooded Sicilian", might find that hard to comprehend since you obviously think with a very different part of your anatomy.'

And that particular part of his anatomy was currently

making its existence felt in the most predictable way possible, Alessio acknowledged wryly. And given that Lindsay Lockheart had yet to discover the wonders of sex without emotional attachment, the only available solution to this particular attack of animal lust appeared to be a cold shower.

'If you have so much faith in your mental discipline, why would you be afraid to come with me?'

'I'm *not* afraid.' Her chin lifted and suddenly the tension between the two of them reached screaming pitch.

'You're afraid, Lindsay,' Alessio said softly, 'and I'll tell you why. So far, the only thing that has kept me from having sex with you is lack of opportunity.'

She was so deliciously easy to shock, he mused, watching as her eyes widened and hot colour poured into her cheeks.

'That's nonsense. We could have all the opportunity in the world and I still wouldn't have—we wouldn't—' She swallowed. 'The ability to think and use our brains is what separates us from animals. I'm in control of what I do.'

'If you're so confident about that, then come in your sister's place.'

He could see a tiny pulse beating in her creamy throat as she struggled with the challenge he'd thrown into her path. 'I can't just abandon my life.'

'You mean you don't trust yourself to be on a Caribbean island with me and not have sex.' He gave a slow, sure smile. 'Be honest, Lindsay. You know that your logical approach to relationships is going to be worth nothing when we're both naked. And you're afraid to lose.'

'Damn you,' she whispered, her eyes sparking angrily. 'Damn you for making this about us when it should be about my sister.'

'If it was about your sister, then you'd come.'

The lawyer in him interpreted every expression that flickered across her face. Nerves, worry, stress, fear and something else that he couldn't immediately identify—something much, much more complex than all the other emotions put together—

'I can't just drop my life at a moment's notice.'

'You're worried that one of your clients might get divorced when you're not looking and that would be bad for publicity?'

'I don't care about publicity. I don't care about winning and losing. I care about people. *I care about Ruby.* And I'm not coming with you.'

Alessio was astonished by the depth of his disappointment.

Why should it matter to him? It wasn't as if his bed was going to be empty.

There was no shortage of beautiful, sophisticated women desperate for his attention. Women who wouldn't waste time fighting him. Why would he be bothered about Lindsay's refusal?

And then he gave a wry smile, a flash of insight giving him the reason for his reaction.

He *hated* losing.

He absolutely hated losing, but it had been so long since he'd lost at anything that he hadn't immediately recognised the feeling. And if there was one thing designed to send his competitive streak into overdrive, it was the concept of losing.

Lindsay Lockheart represented a challenge. And when had a woman ever been a challenge to him?

Aware that his driver was agitated about the time, he applied analytical skills to the problem. 'Fine. If I hear from her before you do I'll be sure to tell her that you cared about her. But not enough to do her job in her place. Have a good flight back.' And with that carefully orchestrated parting shot he strode towards the car, wondering how long it would take.

Three strides? Maybe four?

'All right.' Her voice stopped him on two and he smiled to himself as he turned because in the end it had been disappointingly easy.

Women were so predictable.

'*Scusi?*' He pretended to be confused, watching as she walked towards him like someone going to the gallows.

'Why would you be surprised? You've won, Alessio. Isn't that what you always do? You find your opponent's weakness and you exploit it.' Without giving him time to answer, she pushed past him and slid into the back of the car.

And clearly she wasn't used to getting into the back of a limousine. Accommodating her sudden movement, her skirt slid up to mid-thigh and Alessio's attention was momentarily diverted. *Fabulous legs*, he thought absently, his libido acting like a break on his thought processes. Who would have thought that Lindsay Lockheart was hiding a body like that under her sober, serious black skirt? Those long, shapely legs appeared to be encased in sheer stockings with a hint of a sheen and Alessio found himself wishing that her skirt were just slightly shorter...

Then she tugged the skirt down and Alessio started to breathe again.

'Let me get this straight—' trying to ignore the vicious ache in his loins, he dragged his gaze away from her slender ankles and leaned an arm on the roof of the car '—you're offering to warm my bed in the Caribbean?'

'No, I'm not.' She turned her head and her blue eyes connected with his. 'You may think you've won, but winning doesn't matter to me. All that matters is protecting Ruby. And if stepping into her shoes protects her job, then fine, I'll work for you.' Her tone was cool and collected, but he saw that her pupils were dilated and her breathing was rapid and shallow. Her fingers clutched her bag tightly and Alessio suddenly had a disconcertingly clear image of her naked and squirming on his silk sheets, those same slender fingers curled around a certain part of him.

How much of a nudge would it take to push her from prim to passionate?

He decided to push her a little further out of her comfort zone. 'My client is recovering from the end of a disastrous marriage. He needs relaxation and legal counsel.' *Was she wearing lipstick?* He didn't think so but there was a tempting sheen to her lips. 'A relationship counsellor would be about as helpful on this trip as a blizzard at a barbecue.'

'I'm not accompanying you in my role as relationship counsellor.' She tucked her bag neatly by her side, but still she didn't look at him. 'I worked for a year in a law firm in London when I left college. You can give me a full brief. Whatever it is you expect of Ruby, I'm sure I'll be able to fulfil it. And I *can* relax, Alessio, if that's what's worrying you.' But every angle of her body shrieked tension. She looked like someone who was on the verge of snapping in two.

The trip was clearly going to be a nightmare for her. 'Are you doing this to save your sister's job or to prove to yourself that your brain is stronger than your body?'

She stilled. 'I don't need to prove anything.'

'So it's all about your sister.' But he didn't believe that for a moment. He sensed that there was much, much more behind her acceptance than a desire to protect her sister's job. He also sensed that his careless challenge had touched something deep inside her. 'You think you can make it through a whole week without lecturing me or my client on love and marriage?'

She bit her lip—*the same lip he couldn't stop staring at.* 'Of course.'

'Or sleeping in my bed?'

'That will be the easy part.'

Alessio studied her profile thoughtfully. What had promised to be a mundane, uneventful business trip suddenly seemed full of interesting possibilities. 'What happens when emotions overcome your rational side, Lindsay?'

'Making decisions based on emotions is always a mistake. I don't let that happen.'

Alessio's eyes dropped to the perfect curve of her mouth and drifted down to the slim column of her neck. 'Are you saying that you've never made an impulsive decision based on an emotion?'

'No.' Her tone was crisp. 'And I'm sure that you haven't, either. Even when you're in bed with a woman I'm wiling to bet that part of you stays detached. You exercise control over your emotions all the time and you're much too cynical to allow yourself to be taken for a ride.'

Surprised by her insight, Alessio laughed. 'You might be right about that. All right, Lindsay Lockheart—' he reached out a hand and took the passport she held out to him '—let's see how an incurable cynic and a relationship counsellor get on when confined in a small space. I have a feeling that the next week is going to be interesting.'

Private jet. *Why did he have to own a private jet?*

She'd been hoping for safety in numbers for their flight to the Caribbean, instead of which it was just her and Alessio and a discreet cabin staff who only materialised when something was needed.

Trying not to be overawed by the sumptuous interior of the plane, Lindsay steadily called her way through her list of clients, relieved to have something to do that didn't involve talking to Alessio Capelli. 'I know, Alison,' she soothed as she listened to the latest round of developments in her client's tempestuous marriage, 'but do you remember what we talked about last time we met? About selective listening?' Catching Alessio's amused gaze, she gritted her teeth. 'I'll be back next week and we can talk about it then.' Lindsay ended the conversation and dialled her next number, determined that he wouldn't unsettle her, but all too aware of his own conversation.

'Let her sweat, Jack,' he drawled, the phone tucked between his cheek and his shoulder as he studied the screen of his laptop. 'She'll be lucky to walk away with the staff flat by the time we've finished with her.'

Lindsay gritted her teeth, kept her own call as brief as possible and tried to ignore the worsening pain in her head.

When he finally hung up, she glared at him. 'Don't you ever feel guilty? That poor woman has probably given the best years of her life bringing up his children and making him a home, while he was off picking a younger model.'

Alessio stretched his legs out in front of him, completely relaxed. 'That "poor woman" abandoned her two young children to pursue her affair with her ski instructor.'

Taken aback, Lindsay frowned. 'Oh—that's terrible. The poor man. Is he doing all right?'

'He will be by the time I've finished.' Alessio gave a deadly smile as he pulled a file out of his briefcase. 'Revenge is sweet. We'll get her where it hurts her most.'

Lindsay ignored that comment. 'How are the children?'

'Better off without her.' Alessio opened the file and scribbled something in the margin of the first page while Lindsay watched him, deeply troubled.

'However deep his own pain, I'm sure he wouldn't want to hurt the mother of his children.'

'Are you?' Alessio reached for a file from the table. 'That's why you're not a divorce lawyer.'

Lindsay put down her appointments diary carefully. 'You can't apply cold, hard facts to people's relationships. It just doesn't work. It's important to delve deeper. I'm immediately asking myself why she would do a thing like that. Why would any mother leave her children? Was she depressed or something?'

Alessio gaze was faintly mocking. 'I think it's fair to say that she was *extremely* depressed once she realised that she'd trashed her chance of receiving a generous settlement.'

Lindsay lifted her fingers to her forehead, telling herself

that his warped humour and lack of sentiment was good. If he kept talking like that it would make it easier to ignore the chemistry that still managed to crackle between them. Chemistry that made it impossible for her to relax.

How was she going to survive a week with him?

It wasn't that she had doubts about her own willpower, because she didn't; it was more that their powerful sexual connection stirred up something dark and ugly in the depths of her brain. *Something that she didn't want to face.*

Feeling a flicker of panic, she concentrated her mind on work. 'People usually have reasons for the way they act, Alessio. If she left her children, then—' her hand dropped to her lap as she pondered the issue '—perhaps she didn't want children in the first place. Did he pressure her? Was he a lot older than her? Was parenthood an issue that they discussed before they married?'

Incredulous dark eyes met hers. '*Accidenti*, how would I know? I'm a lawyer, not a psychiatrist.' With an impatient flick of his long fingers, Alessio flipped through the pages.

'But surely they should try some form of counselling before they just give up. He should let her come back and try again. There are children involved—'

'What makes you think she wants to come back?'

Appalled, Lindsay stared at him. 'Doesn't she?'

He lifted his gaze to hers. 'Lindsay—' his voice held a warning note '—you're doing it already. Ignoring the facts and looking at the emotions.'

'Emotions are *important*.'

'But they're *your* emotions,' he pointed out gently, 'not my client's.'

'But the children—'

'You seem particularly sensitive to this situation. Are you this emotionally involved with every case you deal with? No wonder you're always so tense.'

'I'm not tense.' She was agonisingly aware of him, of his powerful shoulders and his hard, handsome face. *Why is it, she wondered desperately, that a person can still be devastatingly attractive even when they are so deficient in other more important qualities?* 'You hate women, don't you?'

He raised an eyebrow. 'Is this my cue to say that some of my best friends are women?'

'That's not friendship.'

His smile was impossibly attractive. 'Friendship means different things to different people.'

And she was in no doubt as to what it meant to him. 'But you seem to make it your life's work to make sure that women don't profit from marriage.'

'Only when the *purpose* of their marriage was profit. I don't believe that marriage should be a source of income.' His long bronzed fingers played idly with his pen and she lifted her own fingers and rubbed her forehead again. The dangerous mix of cool and charismatic was making her head spin.

'It's the source of *your* income,' she pointed out, and his smile widened.

'Touché.' He glanced up as a uniformed girl sashayed down the plane with a tray of refreshments. 'Ah—supper. Are you hungry, Lindsay?'

Her head was getting worse and to make matters worse her stomach was starting to churn. 'Actually, no. But thank you.' She wished once again that she hadn't left her pills at home. This whole situation was going to be difficult enough without having to do it with a headache. 'Perhaps this would be a good time for you to tell me something about the objective of this trip. If I'm to assist you, I'd better know something about the case.'

'My prospective client hasn't yet appointed legal counsel,' Alessio purred. 'He simply wishes to discuss his situation. I've agreed to listen.'

'So he's not even sure he wants a divorce?'

'He knows he wants a divorce—he just hasn't yet decided how to go about it. Or who he wants to represent him.'

'So he might choose you.'

'If he can afford me, he'll choose me.' Alessio suppressed a yawn and Lindsay shot him a bemused glance.

'Why do you do this? You *obviously* don't need the money.'

'I enjoy the mental stimulation. I'm naturally competitive. I enjoy winning.'

'Do you really think it's "winning" to destroy someone's marriage?'

'Marriages come to me ready broken.' His dark eyes flashed a warning. 'And lecturing me isn't in your job description.'

'But has your client even tried to fix what's wrong? Perhaps if he talks to an outsider—someone who isn't involved—' Lindsay broke off and winced as another shaft of pain lanced her head. Her stomach churned horribly and she sat totally still, willing it to settle.

Not now. She didn't need this to happen now.

Alessio frowned, his eyes fixed on her face. 'Is something wrong?'

'Nothing at all.' She could just imagine how a man like him would react to a woman with a migraine. Deciding that it was best to make her escape while she could, she stood up gingerly. 'If you'll excuse me for a moment. I need to use the bathroom.'

His eyes lingered thoughtfully on her face. 'Last door on the left.'

Wishing he weren't studying her quite so intently, Lindsay followed his directions and pushed open a door. Had circumstances been different she would have been amazed by the beautiful bathroom that confronted her, but as it was she felt too ill to react with anything other than relief at the prospect of privacy.

Closing the door carefully behind her, she put her hand on her stomach and took a deep breath. How long was the flight to the Caribbean? She hadn't even asked, but without her medication she knew that she was going to be ill for all of it. And it was going to be horribly embarrassing.

Why now? *Why now, when she really needed to have her wits about her?*

Her head throbbed and she just wanted to lie down, but the thought of doing so in front of Alessio prevented her from returning to the cabin. Instead she sat down on a chair and leaned her head against the cool, marble wall, closing her eyes.

If only the pain would stop—

She didn't know how long she sat there. She was in too much pain to move; so much so that when the bathroom door opened, she barely reacted.

'*Maledizione,*' a rough masculine voice cursed softly, 'how long have you been like this? Are you ill?'

'Migraine. I'll be OK. Just leave me alone for a bit.' Her eyes tightly shut against the light, Lindsay felt a firm masculine hand touch her forehead and then he muttered something under his breath in Italian.

'I thought you were looking pale. Why didn't you say something before?'

'Alessio, please just go away,' she muttered. 'You're difficult enough to deal with in good health. Trust me, you don't want to be in here. I think I might be sick.'

Apparently undeterred by that warning, he scooped her easily into his arms and carried her through a door that led to a bedroom. Then he laid her gently on the enormous king-size bed. The soft pillow was cool against her cheek and it felt so wonderful to lie down that she gave a moan of gratitude.

'Maybe you're not all bad,' she mumbled. 'At this moment in time I almost like you.'

His eyes gleamed. 'Stop talking, Lindsay. You might say something you regret.'

'Sorry. Forgot you don't want women to like you.' She winced as another bolt of pain shot through her head. 'Well, this must be a first for you. Tucking a sick woman into your bed.'

'Do you have tablets in your bag?' He sounded cool and efficient and her eyes drifted shut, her teeth gritted against the pain.

'Forgot them. Packed in a hurry.' She snuggled deeper into the pillow. 'I didn't even know planes came with beds. I guess it's an essential item for a man like you.'

'Believe it or not, I don't use it for seduction. Being able to sleep when I need to makes me more efficient,' he said dryly, pulling a heavy silk cover over her. 'So—what am I going to do with you?'

The pain was agonising and she winced as a shaft of light penetrated the window. 'You're going to pass me my phone. I need to try calling Ruby again—'

'Stop thinking about your sister and think about yourself for once.' A frown in his eyes, Alessio leaned across and closed the blinds, shutting out the beams of sunlight. 'Better?'

She never would have believed him capable of being so thoughtful. But her stomach was still churning and she was terrified that she was going to be sick over his handmade shoes. 'I think you'd better leave now—for your sake.'

It seemed as though he was following her advice because he rose to his feet and left the room. But he returned moments later with a bowl and placed it by the bed, apparently unfazed by the situation. 'I'm going to fetch you a doctor.'

If she'd had more energy Lindsay would have laughed. They were in mid-air, for goodness' sake. Where was he going to find a doctor?

Perhaps he meant that he was going to talk to a doctor on the phone, but what good would that do?

The pounding in her head was unbearable, but when she heard voices next to her she gingerly opened her eyes and saw a man standing with Alessio.

With a frown, he sat down on the bed, asked her a few questions and then opened his bag.

Dimly in the back of her mind Lindsay was wondering how Alessio had managed to produce a doctor in mid-air, but her head was hurting too much to care and she was almost sobbing with gratitude as the doctor gave her medication and then left the room. Moments later, something deliciously cool was placed gently against her throbbing head.

She opened her eyes a slit and saw Alessio sitting next to her. He'd removed his tie and the sleeves of his white shirt had been rolled back to reveal strong forearms shadowed with dark hairs. As always he looked strong and capable and, surprisingly perhaps, not the slightest bit put out by her sudden illness. 'The doctor thought this might help.'

'Thank you. That feels wonderful. Why are you still here?' But she felt intensely vulnerable and pathetically grateful to him for not walking out and leaving her alone. 'I suppose your ego won't allow a woman to claim a headache when she's in your bed.' Her remark made him smile.

'Be quiet and go to sleep, Lindsay.'

'You really are impossibly good-looking,' she muttered as the medication started to take effect and her eyes drifted shut. 'It's a shame you're such a selfish bastard.'

CHAPTER FOUR

SHE woke to find the pain gone and Alessio sprawled on the bed next to her, his eyes closed.

Still sleepy, Lindsay gazed at his dense lashes and the hard lines of his perfect bone structure.

So this was what it felt like to wake up next to a really, *really* gorgeous man. Like not getting up, she thought dreamily. Like spending all day lying in bed staring at him; counting those incredible eyelashes, studying the blue-black stubble that darkened his jaw, following the sensuous curve of his firm mouth.

Even relaxed and asleep, he looked strong and hotly masculine.

She was still in the process of contemplating his mouth when his eyes opened and he looked at her. His gaze locked with hers and for a sizzling moment they shared something agonisingly intimate. The response of her body was instantaneous and without thinking what she was doing, Lindsay lifted a hand and touched his cheek.

She felt the roughness of his jaw against her sensitive palm—man against woman—and then she saw his eyes narrow slightly.

'I gather you're feeling better?' His voice was roughened by sleep, but it was enough to pierce her dreamy state and return her to full consciousness.

Completely awake now, she snatched her hand away and stared at him in horror.

'Oh—' Skidding away from him, she quickly sat up and her hair slid over her shoulders. Only then did she realise that, not only had someone removed the clips from her hair, but they'd also undressed her down to her underwear. She was horribly embarrassed, and her first impulse was to leap from the bed and lock herself in the bathroom, but without clothes she was trapped. Clutching the satin quilt to her throat, she glared at him. 'What are you doing in my bed?'

'It's *my* bed, *tesoro*.' He closed his eyes again and a slight smile played around his firm mouth. *That gorgeous mouth that she'd been examining in such detail.* 'My plane. My bed.'

'But—' she kept the covers up to her chin '—what I mean is—why are you lying next to me?'

'Sorry to disappoint you, but this plane only comes with one bedroom. I don't generally find that I need guest accommodation.'

'You could have slept on the couch.'

'I could have done, yes.' Eyes still closed, he smiled. 'But that would have made me thoughtful and caring, and I'm a selfish bastard, Lindsay. Remember?'

Lindsay tightened her fingers on the covers. 'That was incredibly rude of me. I shouldn't have said that—I'm sorry. I don't know why I did.'

'You were honest about how you felt,' he said dryly, 'I suspect for the first time in your life.'

Lindsay hesitated. 'But I was wrong,' she said quietly. Yes, he'd obviously sprawled next to her for a few hours' sleep, but only after he'd brought a bowl, fetched a doctor and generally made sure that she was as comfortable as possible. 'Who undressed me?'

'I did. I must say, for a relationship counsellor you choose extremely seductive underwear.' He gave a half smile. 'You're full of surprises.'

'You shouldn't have undressed me.'

'I felt sorry for you strapped up in that starched suit. You couldn't possibly get the rest you needed. Is the headache gone?'

She moved her head slightly to test it and then nodded gingerly. 'Yes. Thank you. Where did you find a doctor in mid-air?'

'In the cockpit of my plane.' In no apparent hurry, Alessio sat up, suppressed a yawn and then sprang from the bed with unconscious grace. He strolled to the far side of the bedroom, yanked open a cupboard and removed a fresh shirt. 'My co-pilot is medically trained.'

It didn't matter what he was doing or what he was wearing, he was unfairly good-looking, Lindsay thought helplessly. Whether he was stripped to the waist and sweaty from exercise, sleek in a suit, or rumpled from a few hours' rest on the bed, he still managed to look gorgeous.

With a moan of frustration, she closed her eyes, reminding herself that his looks concealed an ice-cold temperament and a complete lack of emotional intelligence.

But that wasn't quite true, was it?

He could have walked away and left her to her agony, but he hadn't. Nor had he been remotely fazed by the fact that she'd taken ill on his plane. Remembering the glass of water he'd held to her lips at one point, she turned her head into the pillow, terrified by her feelings.

It didn't change a thing, she told herself desperately. All right, so perhaps he did have a human side. But that didn't alter the fact that he didn't believe in love, had no desire to sustain a relationship and made his living from ripping the guts from people's marriages.

It didn't change who he was.

And it didn't change who she was, either. *Didn't change the way she felt inside.*

She opened her eyes and found him looking at her.

'Are you all right?' He frowned. 'Headache back?'

'No. I'm fine.'

'Good. We'll be landing in another two hours. I'm going to take a shower and then make some calls. Help yourself to the bathroom.'

'Wait.' Scooping her hair away from her face, she raised herself on her elbow. 'You haven't even told me where we're going. You just said it was the Caribbean.'

'We're going to Kingfisher Cay, west of Antigua. One hundred acres of isolated palm-fringed beaches and guaranteed isolation.'

'I've never heard of it.'

'The only people who have ever heard of it are the people who can afford to go there,' he said dryly. 'A holiday on Kingfisher Cay is by personal invitation of the owner.'

'And your prospective client is holidaying there as we speak?'

'He needed a rest from the publicity surrounding his disintegrating marriage. He's treating himself to some rest and relaxation.'

'And you're taking advantage of his vulnerability by turning up and offering him legal counsel?'

Alessio gave a cool smile. 'A good divorce lawyer is what makes him able to relax. Without me protecting his interests, he wouldn't be able to risk turning his back on the scheming hussy he married.'

Lindsay's mouth tightened and she gripped the quilt in her fingers. Clearly the thoughtfulness he'd displayed during the night had just been a blip.

'Don't you think the owner of the island might object to you using his exclusive Caribbean hideaway for your own commercial interests?'

'No.' Alessio looked as though something had amused him and she frowned.

'Does he know you're bringing me?'

'Why does it matter?' A dangerous light in his eyes, he strolled purposefully towards her, his smile widening as she retreated to the far side of the bed.

The closer he came, the harder it was to breathe and she felt as though her body were on fire. 'There might not be enough accommodation.'

'We can always share.'

Lindsay flattened herself against the bed head. 'I'd rather sleep with the sharks.'

He stopped, his expression mocking as he registered her growing agitation. 'Then you'd better hope that your little sister did at least one part of her job correctly and booked two suites.' With that disconcerting observation, he turned and walked through to the bathroom, leaving her with a pounding heart and a guilty conscience.

Ruby.

She hadn't even thought about her sister since she'd woken up and she knew why, of course. There had been no room in her brain for anything or anyone except Alessio Capelli.

She needed to call Ruby. She needed—

With a groan, Lindsay flopped back down onto the pillows. What she really needed was to be back in London living her life. *Not* trapped in a private jet, en route to a billionaire's Caribbean hideaway.

The seaplane soared above a sparkling turquoise sea.

'Oh, my goodness,' Lindsay breathed softly, her gaze drawn to yet another emerald-green island surrounded by deserted sandy beaches. 'It's incredible. So beautiful. I had no idea. I've never before understood everyone's obsession with accumulating wealth, but if wealth means seeing a place like this—'

It was idyllic. If it weren't for her anxiety about Ruby, she might even have been able to relax.

Lindsay frowned, realising how ridiculous that was. If it hadn't been for Ruby, she wouldn't be here! And if she started thinking that this was a holiday, she'd be in trouble. The only way to survive a week with Alessio Capelli was to be businesslike.

Absorbed by the contents of the file on his lap, Alessio appeared unaware of her inner turmoil. 'You've never been to the Caribbean?'

'No, I—' She broke off. She didn't want to reveal anything about herself to this man. What would someone like him make of her disordered, disastrous childhood? He'd laugh or make one of his sharp, lawyerlike comments that always made her shrink. 'I haven't really travelled.' Not wanting to think about her past, she peered down at the surf breaking on a beach below her. 'Is that where we're going?'

'Yes.' Unlike her, he hadn't once glanced out of the window, instead concentrating on working his way through the thick sheaf of documents. Occasionally he scribbled a note in the margin, sometimes he underlined, rarely he frowned and crossed out a chunk of text with big, bold strokes of his black pen.

Did he ever relax? She studied his profile for a moment. He'd showered and shaved and was now dressed in light-weight trousers and a cool shirt.

'Why do you work so hard? Is it all about the money?' She blurted out the question and he lifted his head and looked at her.

'Money is important up to a point. After that, the amount becomes irrelevant.'

Lindsay tried to imagine having so much money that the total became irrelevant. 'Well, you've long passed that point,' she muttered, 'so why do you carry on?'

'Because it entertains me.' He slid his pen into his pocket and closed the file. 'I enjoy the process.'

'You mean you enjoy making people miserable.'

His eyes gleamed. 'On the contrary, I free them from misery to begin a new life.'

'Don't you ever worry that you've taken apart something that could be fixed?'

'Unlike you, I don't feel the need to control everybody else's actions. If someone comes to me seeking legal advice, I give it. I don't try and persuade them that they're wrong.'

'But what if some of those marriages could be saved? Perhaps some of those poor children could be spared the misery of spending their lives shuttling backwards and forwards every other weekend.'

Alessio slipped the file into his briefcase and snapped it shut. 'You're extremely concerned about the children in every relationship.'

Her heart thudded against her chest. It really wouldn't pay to underestimate this man. He was *so* astute. 'Of course. Who wouldn't be?' She gave a humourless laugh. 'Sorry—you're not at all concerned, are you?'

'I think a bad relationship can be every bit as damaging for children as a split family.'

'But what if the bad relationship could be fixed?'

'You're ridiculously sentimental about everything and you take it far too personally.' His gaze was suddenly thoughtful. 'Or maybe it *is* personal. Is it personal, Lindsay? Or do you feel this strongly on every subject?'

Her mouth dried. 'I care, that's all.'

'I know. I'm just wondering why.'

'Because I'm a human being.' Deeply regretting ever starting the conversation, Lindsay concentrated her attention on the Caribbean Sea, which sparkled beneath her in the dazzling sunlight. She'd forgotten that he was a lawyer. With a few simple words he'd turned everything around and suddenly she was the one in the dock.

She needed to be careful.

Really careful.

'So what do you want me to do?' Realising that they'd finally arrived, she turned to him. 'I mean, I expect you were planning to brief me on the flight, but I was ill—do you have something I should read? What's my role?'

He circled a word on the page in front of him and then looked up. 'Your role, Lindsay, is to act as my assistant.' His dark eyes held hers for a moment and she felt everything inside her grow warm.

Appalled by her extremely unwelcome reaction to him, she frowned and dragged her gaze from his. 'I know that I'm your assistant, but I'm just not sure what you expect of me. Some details would be helpful.'

'I expect you to make our client feel comfortable. We need to make him feel that we understand his situation and that we're committed to representing his interests.'

'All right.'

'I don't expect you to ask if he's tried counselling.'

Lindsay swallowed. 'Fine. Are you going to tell me about him?'

'Not yet. His presence on the island is top secret. If his identity was leaked, it could cause a problem. The owner prides himself on guaranteeing the absolute discretion of everyone on the island.'

'But he trusts you?'

'Lindsay—' his voice was gentle '—I *am* the owner. It's my island.'

'Yours?' She looked at him stupidly and then out of the window at the sugar-soft sandy beach that stretched towards a stylish beachfront villa. Another villa was visible farther along the sand. 'You own this? I thought you were a lawyer, not a property magnate.'

'I have several business interests.' He slid the file into his briefcase.

Lindsay arched an eyebrow. 'Worried that the divorce business might not sustain you into your old age, Alessio?'

'It's good business practice to diversify and I find my various business interests complement each other. You'd be surprised how many men are eager to check into remote, five-star luxury in order to escape their marriages.'

'Escape responsibility, you mean.'

Alessio gave a faint smile. 'As I was saying, Kingfisher Cay fits nicely into my business portfolio. The rich and famous are guaranteed an exclusive hideaway in which they can lick their wounds, safe in the knowledge that the world's press aren't watching them.'

'And safe in the knowledge that their exclusive private villa comes with free legal advice.'

'I wouldn't exactly describe it as "free".' Alessio leaned across and unfastened her seat belt, his eyes settling on her black skirt. 'I have a feeling that the first thing you might want to do is rethink your wardrobe. You're going to be extremely hot in that suit.' He was uncomfortably close to her and although she wanted desperately to look away, somehow she couldn't quite manage it. It was as if he were holding her there, trapped. Helpless. Something flickered in the depths of his eyes, something raw and elemental, and her heart started to bump rapidly against her chest.

'I have a change of clothes in my bag,' she said hoarsely, but still he didn't move, the temperature between them rising to intolerable levels as he held her gaze.

Then he released his own seat belt and stood up. 'Good.'

She thought he was smiling, but she couldn't be sure because he was talking to the pilot in rapid Italian and then the door of the plane opened and sunlight and warmth filled the cabin.

Alessio turned, his hair gleaming blue-black under the burning sun, more shockingly handsome than any man had a right to be. 'Welcome to Kingfisher Cay.'

So he was handsome, she'd always known that.

Damn the man.

Feeling hot, sticky and desperately unsettled, Lindsay dumped her small overnight bag on the floor of the villa and burst out laughing. When Alessio had told her she would be staying in a villa she'd imagined that she'd be sharing something relatively modest with several other people. Instead, the smiling staff member who had met their seaplane had led her to a private villa. A villa just for her. And her overnight bag looked as out of place as she felt.

The spacious living room opened directly onto the beach and was decorated in a sophisticated palette of cool colours that created an atmosphere of restful calm. The bedroom was dominated by an enormous teak four-poster bed, draped in acres of light creamy muslin and dressed with piles of silk cushions in elegant, restrained shades.

Lindsay stared around her in disbelief, so distracted by her surroundings that she forgot she was hot, sticky and desperately uncomfortable. She forgot about the hot burn of sexual awareness that had been with her ever since she'd arrived at Alessio's office. She even forgot that she still hadn't managed to contact Ruby. She was so stunned by the sheer luxury of the villa that for a moment she simply stood there.

What was she doing here?

Had this really been Ruby's life? It was hardly surprising she'd loved her job if this was one of the perks.

She strolled through a door and found herself in a lavish marble bathroom that again opened directly onto the beach. Taking in the multispray shower and the array of exclusive toiletries, Lindsay shook her head.

It was possible to lie in the bath and stare at the palm trees swaying on the beach.

If staying here was work, what did Alessio Capelli do for entertainment?

Hearing footsteps behind her, she turned and saw a pretty blonde girl dressed in a white uniform standing in the doorway.

'I'm Natalya. I'm your housekeeper for the duration of your stay at Kingfisher Cay. Anything you want, you have only to ask. I expect you're hot and tired after your journey. Would you like to change while I unpack for you?'

Unpack? Unpack what, exactly?

Lindsay's eyes slid to her bag. It sat forlorn and abandoned in the centre of the polished wooden floor. 'I don't have much luggage. I wasn't expecting— This was a bit of an—impulse trip.'

As if anyone would come to a place like this on impulse. Even for the elite few fortunate enough to be able to afford it, it would be a rare treat. For the rest of the population, the silky sand and turquoise sea of Kingfisher Cay would never be more than a picture to drool over in an exotic travel brochure. Except that this place didn't feature in travel brochures.

Natalya didn't appear to find the absence of luggage at all odd. Obviously accustomed to the odd behaviour of the rich and famous, she simply smiled. 'We pride ourselves in being able to provide anything and everything you need. If you like, you can give me a list. Or I can simply provide you with what I think you'll need for a happy and comfortable stay here.'

Lindsay smiled at that. 'You're even prepared to do my thinking for me?'

'We're used to living here,' Natalya murmured. 'We know what you're likely to need.'

'I don't want to put you to any trouble. I'm sure you have plenty of other guests.' More important guests.

'We have a staff ratio of eight to one.'

'One member of staff for eight guests?' Lindsay was thinking that seemed like a lot when the girl smiled.

'Eight members of staff for each guest.'

Stunned into silence, Lindsay simply gaped at her. 'Oh—'

'Signor Capelli asked that you meet him at the Beach Club for a drink in twenty minutes.'

'Right.' Lindsay looked at her helplessly. 'And where is that, exactly?'

'If you come to the front of your villa when you're ready, I'll direct you.'

Alessio nursed his drink and stared moodily at the smooth turquoise ocean as he contemplated the case. He wasn't surprised that the 'A' list Hollywood star wanted a divorce. What surprised him was that the man had been foolish enough to marry his co-star in the first place.

She had 'opportunist' written all over her particularly stunning face.

What was it about a beautiful woman that turned otherwise sensible men into fools?

A yacht drifted across his line of vision, the sails providing an elaborate splash of colour against the endless blue.

'Alessio?'

Irritated at being disturbed, he turned his head and found himself staring straight into the grave, serious eyes of Lindsay Lockheart.

Hovering awkwardly in her sensible navy skirt and tailored shirt, she looked as out of place as a sparrow suddenly finding itself in the midst of a flock of exotic birds.

Controlling or not, she must really love her sister, Alessio mused as he acknowledged just how uncomfortable she was and how little she evidently wanted to be here.

'I thought you were going to change.'

'I *did* change.' Startled, she glanced down at herself, as if checking that her clothes hadn't suddenly disappeared. 'This is a different outfit.'

Alessio contemplated the formal navy skirt with a mixture of exasperation and amusement. 'Clearly you consider it prudent to always be ready for a funeral.'

Soft colour highlighted her cheekbones. 'I'm dressed for work. I gave a television interview in London just before I flew to see you in Rome. *Obviously* at the time I didn't know I was going to need clothes for a warm climate.'

On the surface she appeared brisk and businesslike, but as she pulled out the chair opposite and sat down Alessio noticed the tremor in her hands. And she wasn't quite meeting his eyes. Instead she placed her notepad on the table in front of her and opened it, clearly relieved to have something to focus on that didn't include him. 'Right. Let's get started.'

Unable to resist the opportunity to tease her, Alessio lounged back in his chair. 'What, no foreplay?'

Her gaze flew to his and a flash of sexual awareness darkened her eyes from blue to indigo.

Watching her reaction, Alessio saw the exact moment that she rejected that response. She took several breaths and her fingers tightened on the pen.

Ignoring his comment, she wrote the date neatly and carefully at the top of the pad. 'I thought it would be sensible to take some notes on what you want me to do.'

She just blocked it out, he mused silently. This sizzling chemistry between them was something that she just tried to ignore.

'Efficient, Lindsay. Always in control. Tell me something—' fascinated by the tiny pulse in her slender neck, he studied her for a long moment '—do you ever do anything on impulse?'

'Coming here was an impulsive action,' she responded instantly. 'I hadn't planned to spend the next week on a Caribbean island with a—' She broke off and he raised an eyebrow.

'You were saying? With a—?'

'I'm here in place of my sister, so that you don't have reason to fire her. Talking of which, have you managed to contact your brother?'

'I haven't tried.' Alessio swivelled his gaze to one of the bar staff, who immediately produced two refreshing cocktails filled with crushed ice and topped with exotic fruit. 'Have a drink. You need to relax.'

She ignored the drink. 'Why?'

'Because too much tension is bad for your health.'

She frowned impatiently. 'I mean, why haven't you tried to contact your brother? You promised that you would.'

'I've already left one message.'

'Then leave another. Keep ringing until he answers!'

'What would be the point of that? He'll respond when he's ready.' Watching her body language, Alessio reached for his drink. 'Are you always this wound up? Your blood pressure must be sky-high.'

'I'm not wound up.' But even the way she was sitting shrieked of tension. She perched on the edge of her chair, her back straight and her hands on the pad in front of her, ready to take notes.

'Do you even know how to relax? Or is it just that you're afraid to relax with me?' It was as if she was watching herself all the time, using iron willpower to make sure that she didn't slip up.

'I relax when the time is appropriate. This isn't that time. So what's happening with your client?' She was brisk and business-like, her blonde hair drawn back from her face, her shirt buttoned almost to the throat. 'What time are we meeting him?'

'I have no idea. He hasn't arrived.'

Exasperation shone in her eyes. 'So, when is he coming?'

'When it suits him.'

'You haven't asked?'

Alessio smiled. 'I'm sure he'll arrive when he's ready.'

'But you've adjusted your working schedule to accommodate him—'

'And he's paying me for the privilege,' Alessio drawled softly. 'How he chooses to use my time is entirely up to him. In the meantime we're free to—relax and get to know each other better.' He saw the movement in her throat as she swallowed.

'I don't want to get to know you better. I already know you well enough.'

'But didn't you say that it was important to delve deeper?'

'You're twisting my words.'

'I'm merely playing your own words back to you.'

She turned her head and looked at the ocean, but he could see the desperation in her eyes and she took several small breaths before turning back to him. 'If you don't need me to work immediately then perhaps you could lend me the file and I'll go back to the villa and make some notes. At least then I'll be prepared when he finally turns up. I can sign a confidentiality agreement if you think it's necessary.'

He wondered what it would take to get her out of that navy skirt and away from her legal pad. 'Do you sail?'

'Sorry?' She looked startled. 'Why are you asking that?'

'Because we need to find a way of passing the time until my client arrives. I have other suggestions, of course...' Alessio allowed his sentence to remain unfinished, enjoying the confusion in her eyes.

'I don't need you to entertain me.' Apparently that last remark was sufficient to make her reach for her drink. Lifting it to her lips, she took a large sip and then put the glass carefully back down on the table. 'If you have no immediate need for me, I'll just stay in my villa and take the odd swim. You carry on and do whatever it is you usually do when you're here.' Her tight voice suggested that she knew exactly what his usual form of entertainment was, and Alessio laughed.

'You're going to swim?'

'Why is that funny?'

'Because I've never seen anyone swimming in a navy skirt before. And you seem determined not to be parted from yours.'

'Don't be ridiculous.'

'I just can't imagine you relaxing enough to strip off.'

'I've already told you—I'm perfectly capable of relaxing, Alessio.'

He studied her for a moment wondering what it was about her that was holding his attention. 'In that case go and change out of those warm winter clothes and have a dip in the sea. I'll pick you up at eight o'clock for dinner.'

'I don't have anything to change into.'

'My staff will have rectified that by now, I'm sure.' He'd given them an exact brief on what he wanted and now he was waiting with interest to see how Lindsay reacted to her new wardrobe. He had a feeling that the clothes she wore were part of her defence.

What would happen to her rigid control when she was no longer protected by the comforting security of navy blue or black?

She was convinced she had the mental strength to resist the chemistry between them.

Alessio suddenly discovered just how much he was looking forward to proving her wrong.

CHAPTER FIVE

LINDSAY stared at her reflection in despair.

When she'd returned to the villa to find the wardrobe stocked with a wide selection of summery clothes, she'd been relieved and grateful.

Reluctant though she'd been to admit as much to Alessio, she was *boiling* and had been finding her skirt scratchy and uncomfortable in the shimmering Caribbean heat.

Relief had turned to amazement as she'd examined the contents of her new wardrobe more closely.

Unaccustomed to such a degree of luxury, she was woman enough to feel a flare of excitement as she'd rifled through the dresses on the rail and sifted her way through beautifully folded tops and cardigans, all separated by tissue paper to minimise creasing. And it hadn't just been clothes. There were shoes, all in her size, bags, accessories and a basket heaped with a selection of exclusive make-up, all new and still in the packaging.

But her laughter had faded as soon as she'd realised that none of the clothes was what she would have chosen. It was true that neither of the two skirts she had with her was suitable for a week on a Caribbean Island. For a start they were just too hot and, yes, she'd be the first to agree that they were also too formal.

But there was informal and then there was—romantic. *Romantic and sexy.* And the entire wardrobe that had been provided for her seemed to fall into that category. She'd spent half an hour rifling through the rail over and over again, searching for something that said 'work in a warm climate'. But everything in front of her just seemed to shriek 'take me, take me'.

The options had either been too short, too fitted, too low cut, or too dressy.

One dress in particular had caught her attention and she'd looked at it in despair, knowing that only an extremely sexually confident woman would dare to wear strapless, scarlet silk.

She certainly wasn't that woman.

Which was why, in the end, she'd opted for the turquoise dress.

It shimmered in the light and had clearly been lovingly created by some top designer with seduction in mind.

It wasn't quite as terrifying as the wicked scarlet dress, but it still made her feel uncomfortable.

How could she possibly join a man like Alessio Capelli for dinner wearing something like this?

It was asking for trouble.

For a start it was semi-transparent, presumably designed to be worn over glamorous underwear on an intimate occasion. Or possibly over a swimsuit, by someone so wealthy that shockingly expensive silk could be regarded as beachwear.

The rest of the wardrobe was much the same. Brightly coloured tops, beach dresses, long floating skirts—everything achingly feminine and designed for an ultra-romantic holiday.

But she wasn't on holiday.

And knowing Alessio Capelli—*knowing his ego and his arrogance*—if she wore these clothes, he'd take it as a sign that she wanted to take their relationship a step further.

It was incredibly generous of him to have provided her with a suitable wardrobe, but—

Her eyes narrowed as a sudden thought struck her.

Generous? Was he being generous? Or was he testing her in some way?

Remembering the way he'd teased her, she suddenly realised that it was far more likely that there was a deeper, darker reason for the choice of clothes.

Angry with herself for being so naïve, she glared at her reflection in the mirror.

This wasn't generosity on his part.

He *wanted* her to feel uncomfortable.

He *wanted* her out of her depth.

Apparently he found the unfortunate chemistry between them entertaining and he didn't bother to pretend otherwise. But nor was he allowing her to pretend. He was upfront and straight about the attraction.

And she was honest enough with herself to admit that she was on dangerous ground. Alessio wasn't a man that women could easily ignore. He was, quite simply, the most devastatingly attractive man she'd ever met. Sinfully handsome, he had a way of looking at a woman that made her think of nothing but sex.

And it wasn't just looks. If it had been, perhaps she would have found him easier to resist, but his sharp intelligence made him stimulating company and she was finding it impossible to forget how kind he'd been to her on the plane when she'd been ill.

That kindness had been all the more surprising given his reputation.

If she was honest, the chemistry between them was starting to terrify her.

She, of all people, knew the dangers of that degree of chemistry—*she knew just how easy it was to confuse overwhelming physical attraction with something deeper*. And yet, even knowing that, her body still hummed and simmered and responded to the lazy, suggestive glint in his eyes.

And she didn't want that. Dear God, she really, *really* didn't want that.

She'd seen where that could lead.

Feeling intensely vulnerable and incredibly alone, Lindsay sank down on the edge of the bed and forced herself to do something that she never usually allowed herself to do.

She thought about her childhood.

Instead of blocking out those memories, she allowed them to filter through to her brain. What started as a trickle became a flood, and for a brief, horrible moment she was a little girl again, curled up in her tiny bed with her younger sister asleep in her arms. And she was listening to the sounds through the wall. Those sounds.

The sounds she hated.

The sounds that meant that her father would be coming back home for a while. 'It's all right, Lindsay, we'll be a family again. Everything is going to be different now.'

Breathing rapidly, Lindsay rose to her feet, slamming the lid back down on her thoughts, appalled at how quickly she could regress from competent professional to needy child.

She was well aware of how vulnerable the needy child was. Look at Ruby. There was no doubt in her mind that her mixed up little sister flitted from one relationship to another because she was looking for the love and security she hadn't had as a child.

Impatient with herself, Lindsay paced barefoot into the bathroom.

But she wasn't going to do that.

Sex wasn't love.

Sex wasn't security.

Sex was just—well, sex.

Turning on the taps, she leaned over the washbasin, filled her palms with cold water and splashed her face as if washing her face might also wash away the memories that she'd conjured up.

It had only been a brief glimpse, but it was enough.

Enough to strengthen her resolve.

With the cool water came a feeling of calm and she blotted her face with a towel and stared in the mirror.

It didn't matter what dress she chose to wear. It wasn't going to make a difference to who she was or how she'd chosen to live her life. She was never, ever going to let sexual chemistry cloud her judgment.

Never. It just wasn't going to happen. No matter how sexy the man. No matter what the temptation.

Having seen first-hand the devastation that such a relationship caused, there was no way she was going to make that mistake herself. And wearing a sexy dress and a pair of gorgeous shoes wasn't going to change that.

She made decisions with her head and her brain, not with her body.

It didn't matter that she was in paradise with a dangerously sexy man and a wardrobe to die for.

She was still using her brain. She was still in charge of her decisions.

She could wear any one of those sexy dresses and it wouldn't make a difference to the outcome of the evening.

'Let's see which one of us suffers most, Alessio Capelli,' she murmured under her breath as she selected a lip gloss from the basket of make-up that had been left for her use. Removing it from its packaging, she applied it to her lips and stared at herself with satisfaction.

Clothes and make-up didn't dictate your choices in life.

She could be naked and she'd still be able to resist Alessio Capelli because that was what she wanted to do.

It was all about choices and she knew which choice she was going to make.

Alessio strolled up to the open door of the villa and paused, stunned by the vision that confronted him.

The door was open and he watched transfixed as Lindsay—

a vastly different Lindsay—twisted her hair into a knot and fastened it with a clasp made from a seashell.

Her slender form shimmered in turquoise silk, an exotic vision of femininity. His gaze lingered on the curve of her bottom and he felt an instantaneous surge of lust.

'Well—' without waiting for an invitation, he strolled into the living room '—you clearly didn't have a problem finding something to wear in the wardrobe.'

And he'd expected her to. In fact he'd prepared himself for protests. But there was no protest. Instead she appeared almost serene.

'Why would I have had a problem?' Tilting her head, she checked her reflection in the mirror, as composed and controlled as ever. 'It's incredibly generous of you to lend me so many beautiful things. Thank you, Alessio.' With a smile that appeared genuine, she slid her feet into a pair of sparkling jewelled shoes with heels so high that walking should have been impossible.

Scanning the length of her legs, Alessio was forced to admit that, yet again, Lindsay Lockheart had surprised him. He hadn't expected a positive reaction to the wardrobe he'd provided. He'd instructed the staff to select glamorous clothes, designed to accommodate the needs of a relaxed woman on a beach holiday.

Lindsay wasn't anyone's idea of a relaxed woman.

Knowing what he knew about her desire to control every aspect of her life, he was astonished that she'd apparently embraced someone else's choice of clothes—particularly when those clothes were a dramatic departure from her normal choice of dress. He had a strong suspicion that dressing in a boring and businesslike fashion was all part of her desperate urge to control her surroundings and the way everyone reacted to her. That being the case, he would have expected her to be uncomfortable parted from her crisp white shirt and her safe navy skirt. Instead she was reacting to her new look with decidedly feminine enjoyment.

Far from rejecting the clothes, she seemed to be revelling in them.

His experienced eye noted the subtle touches of make-up that drew attention to her soft, lush mouth and her smooth creamy skin.

And then something in her eyes caught his attention—a cool unspoken challenge that was at odds with a woman who was dressing up purely for pleasure.

And he knew then that she wasn't relaxed.

He smiled to himself, deriving a certain satisfaction from the fact that he'd read her correctly after all. She wasn't at all relaxed. But she was determined that he wouldn't know it.

So why was she wearing the clothes?

Why wasn't she standing in front of him demanding that he find her a navy linen suit or something else designed to extinguish the last burning embers of a man's libido?

'Has your client arrived?' Still focusing on her reflection, she pushed a few wisps of blonde hair away from her face.

'Not yet.'

'Clearly he has money to burn.' Lindsay turned to face him. 'I'm sure you'll charge him for your time, whether he turns up or not.'

'Of course.'

They were sustaining a conversation and yet an entirely different form of communication was simmering beneath the surface of cool civility. With his skill at reading women, Alessio noted the slight flush in her cheeks that had nothing to do with the application of make-up and the darkening of her eyes.

Dealing with his own burn of lust, he wondered how long they were going to play this game.

'I still haven't managed to contact Ruby.'

He had a feeling she'd raised the subject of her sister purely to remind him of the reason she was here.

'That doesn't surprise me. If she wanted you to know where she is, she would have told you.'

Alessio felt the vicious tug of lust deep in his loins because she looked truly beautiful and something about the way she was looking at him drove every rational thought from his head.

'Something wrong, Alessio?' She raised an eyebrow and he smiled in response, well aware that she'd won that round.

Suffer, her eyes were saying and he almost laughed because he *was* suffering and he was completely sure that she knew it.

For a brief moment he contemplated backing her against the enormous bed and removing the dress he'd paid for, but he knew that such an unsubtle approach would just give her opportunity to reject him.

So instead he satisfied himself with a long, lazy look at her.

The colour of the dress was perfect for her skin and hair; turquoise shot with strands of blue and green, the dress fell from tiny beaded straps and was cut to display the tempting dip between her breasts. Alessio's appreciative gaze lingered on the hollow cleft and he heard her sharp intake of breath.

'Do you think you could remove your eyes from my cleavage?'

He smiled. 'Why would I want to do that? You look spectacular.'

'Thank you.' She accepted the compliment in a business-like fashion and walked briskly towards the door. Only once she'd created a safe distance between them, did she turn. 'Are you coming?'

Alessio strolled towards her and tucked her hand into the crook of his arm, feeling a flicker of satisfaction as he felt her initial resistance.

He knew that she was nowhere near as cool and indifferent as she was pretending to be.

But instead of withdrawing or arguing, she simply smiled again. 'I'm looking forward to dinner. What are the local delicacies?'

You are, my beauty, Alessio thought, steering her through a lush tropical garden and down onto the silky white sand. *You're going to be my starter, main course and dessert.*

Lindsay sat down at the table, trying not to show how disconcerted she was that they were dining alone on the private beach in front of the villa.

'This is nice,' she lied. Silver cutlery glinted in the late evening sunlight, a bunch of colourful tropical blooms formed the centrepiece of the table and several candles flickered in the gentle breeze. With the soft sound of the sea licking the shore, it was idyllic, romantic and totally inappropriate for their relationship. The clothes had been bad enough, but this—

This was the setting for seduction, not business. For lovers, not colleagues.

Another test?

Was he putting her through this on purpose?

She cast what she hoped was a casual glance in his direction, but he was as cool and controlled as ever, his handsome face revealing absolutely nothing of his thoughts. Instead he watched her with those dark eyes that she suspected saw far too much.

'I would have thought you would have preferred to dine in the restaurant.' Pleased with how relaxed she sounded, she reached for the cocktail.

'We could have dined in the Beach Club, but this is more— intimate…' he paused and the word hung in the air between them, heating the atmosphere and raising the tension '…and I know you're a real fan of intimacy, Lindsay.'

'Absolutely.' But not with him. The last thing she wanted or needed was intimacy with Alessio Capelli.

'You seem a little tense.'

Tense? *Tense?*

Her entire body was being overtaken by a ferocious sexual awareness and the feeling totally unsettled her. She really, really didn't want to feel like this. 'Why would I be tense? Who could possibly be tense in a place like this?' Nervously looking for something to do with her hands, she leaned forward to help herself to a canapé and saw his eyes drift down to her cleavage.

Immediately she sat back in her chair, her skin heating as he gave a soft smile.

'You don't like the look of the canapés? I can instruct the staff to bring a different selection.'

'Not at all. I decided to save myself for the main course.' Hoping desperately that the staff would serve her, Lindsay struggled with the urge to glance down and check she was decent. She badly wanted to haul her dress up to her neck. It was one thing to be full of bravado when she was staring at her reflection in the mirror, and quite another to maintain that feeling when confronted by a man of Alessio's sophistication and experience.

She suspected that he was playing with her and his next action confirmed it.

A faint smile on his hard mouth, he reached forward and selected a canapé for himself. 'I find that the right taste on the palate actually increases the appetite.' With a slow, deliberate flick of his tongue, he devoured the tiny pastry. 'Sort of culinary foreplay.'

Her heart was thumping hard. 'So you even think about sex when you eat.'

'Sex and food are closely related. Each requires the full involvement of the senses and each satisfies a basic human need.'

Lindsay was desperately conscious of the slow build of warmth low in her pelvis and suddenly she was angry with him—*angry with him for making her feel this way.*

Obviously he thought that the clothes and the setting would guarantee the outcome he wanted.

Well, she was about to show him how wrong he was about her.

'Those canapés do look delicious,' she said sweetly. 'Maybe I will try one after all.' She leaned forward again and this time she made no attempt to prevent her dress from offering what she was sure was a generous glimpse of cleavage.

Without once glancing in his direction, she nibbled at the corner of a pastry and then gave a soft moan and licked her lips. 'That,' she murmured softly, 'tastes absolutely sublime.' Closing her eyes, she slowly slid the rest of the morsel between her lips and chewed slowly. Then she opened her eyes and looked straight at him, challenge in her gaze.

His eyes were black and deadly and held hers for a long, disturbing moment. His long, bronzed fingers toyed idly with the stem of his wineglass and she felt a wicked, delicious curl of excitement low in her belly as the tension between them rocketed to the point of explosion.

'You look warm, Alessio.' Her voice calm and steady, she reached for the refreshing cocktail that had been placed by her plate. 'Is something wrong?'

His eyes held hers for a long, pulsing moment and when he finally spoke his voice was husky with the sizzling tension that was bubbling up between them. 'I hope you know what you're doing.'

'What am I doing? Simply enjoying the food and the sur-roundings.' And proving to herself that she was in control. *That she could resist this man.* 'Presumably that's what you intended when you set this up. Or did you have something else in mind, Alessio?'

'You're playing with fire, *tesoro*,' he warned softly, 'and you're going to be burned.'

'Fire is perfectly safe as long as you know how to handle it.'

His gaze didn't shift from hers. 'Perhaps that depends on the heat of the flame.'

Sure of herself—*proud of herself*—Lindsay smiled. 'You're hot, Alessio,' she said calmly, 'but you're not *that* hot.'

'No? So why can't you stop thinking about sex? Why are you sitting there trying to wipe out images of the two of us together in that enormous canopied bed?'

She gave a tiny gasp, but there was no emotion in his cool gaze, just a glimmer of masculine satisfaction that showed her that, no matter how hard she tried to shift the balance, he still had the upper hand.

'Your misplaced degree of confidence in yourself must mean that you're often disappointed.'

'I'll tell you whether I'm disappointed when you're naked underneath me and I'm deep inside you.'

'I can't believe you just said that.' Lindsay rose to her feet, knocking her drink over in the process.

With supersonic reflexes, a lean, bronzed hand shot out and caught the glass, preventing a spillage.

'What can't you believe? The fact that I thought it? Or the fact that I said it?' Suddenly he had the upper hand again and she lifted a hand to her throat, feeling her pulse racing under the tips of her fingers.

His words had created a vivid image that she couldn't dismiss from her head. An image she'd been trying hard not to look at.

'For a supposedly highly intelligent male, you're extremely narrow-minded.'

'I'm honest. I'm telling you what I'm thinking. Sit down, Lindsay. You've been goading me all evening. You can't expect me not to respond.'

'Not every man is as obsessed with sex as you.'

He lifted an eyebrow. 'Lindsay, I'm a normal, red-blooded male with a healthy sex drive. I've never denied that. You've been sucking your fingers, moaning with pleasure and flashing your gorgeous breasts at me for the last half hour. What did you expect?'

'I expected the reaction I got.' She sat back down, her gaze wary. 'Which just goes to show that despite your intelligence, you think with your hormones and not your brain. Which in turn explains why you've never sustained a relationship outside the bedroom.'

'I've never sustained a relationship outside the bedroom because that's been my choice.'

'What are you afraid of, Alessio?' If she hadn't been watching carefully she might have missed his reaction because it was swiftly controlled.

Controlled, but definitely there.

'Do I look afraid?'

'I think you've *learned* to hide how you feel. You're afraid you won't be able to control your emotions, so you make sure that you don't engage them.' Why, oh, why, had she ever thought she'd be able to cope with this man? 'We're very different, Alessio. Just accept it.'

'I accept that we're different. It's the differences that excite me.' His voice was silky soft and seductive. 'I think we'd be hot in bed. And you think it too, don't you, Lindsay? That's why you're fighting it every step of the way. This chemistry between us is so powerful that you're afraid you're being sucked in. You want to be in control, but even while you're reaching for your drink you're wondering how it's going to feel when I finally kiss you.'

Her mouth was so dry she could barely form the words. 'You're *not* going to kiss me.'

'I am.' He dropped his gaze to her mouth, his tone faintly apologetic. 'When I want something, I have to have it. It's part of my personality.'

Lindsay reached for her drink. 'You could talk to a trained

counsellor about that. You might find that a course of cognitive behavioural therapy might help.'

'I find it's simpler just to take what I want.' He gave a careless shrug of his broad shoulders. 'It's going to happen, Lindsay. Stop fighting it.'

Lindsay carefully put down her drink. Her hand was shaking so much it was that or spill it.

Before she could respond, the several waiters arrived with a tempting platter heaped with fresh seafood, bowls of salad and hot crusty bread.

As the food was served she was aware of Alessio watching her. Could he see? Could he see that her fingers shook when she picked up her fork? Could he see that she was in turmoil?

When they were alone again, she lifted her head and looked him in the eye, banishing visions of his bronzed, naked body covering hers. 'I'm prepared to perform whatever tasks you expected of Ruby. I'm quite sure that providing you with bedroom entertainment wasn't one of them.'

'There has never been any chemistry between us.'

'And that's all it takes to establish a relationship from your point of view? Chemistry?' Her laugh was tinged with derision. 'That's deep, Alessio. I'm sure your past encounters have been extremely—satisfying.'

'I make sure that they are.'

'I'm not talking about sexual satisfaction. I'm talking about something far deeper and more long lasting than that.' There was a cooling breeze from the sea but she still felt desperately hot. 'You're an intelligent man. Surely you demand more from a woman than the ability to simply lie down in your bed.'

'Absolutely.' Alessio didn't shift his eyes from her face. 'I demand a great deal more than that. And I'm sure you'll deliver.'

Was it her or had the temperature on the beach suddenly gone up? 'You shouldn't reduce every relationship to the physical.'

'You shouldn't dismiss sexual satisfaction until you've tried it.'

'What makes you think I haven't?'

'Because you're inexperienced.'

'You know nothing about my private life. Nor do I intend to discuss it with you.'

'Lindsay—' his tone was gentle '—you've been teasing and tempting me since the moment I arrived at your villa this evening. I don't know whether you're trying to prove something to yourself, but only someone *very* inexperienced would play those sorts of games with someone like me.'

'I'm not playing games.'

'I haven't quite worked out if you're a virgin or not,' he murmured, his strong fingers closing around the stem of his glass. 'You're certainly a bit old to be a virgin, but if you've had sex with anyone before, then I'm guessing that it was an instantly forgettable experience. And at this precise moment you're feeling very, very unsettled because you know that sex with me would be a completely *unforgettable* experience.'

Finally she lifted her head and looked at him. 'You're so arrogant.'

'You know we'll be good together, but you're afraid to admit it.'

'That isn't what's happening here at all! I'm not denying that you're attractive, of course you are. Nor am I denying that there's a certain—' she swallowed '—chemistry between us. But the reason I'm not acting on it has nothing to do with fear. It's a choice, Alessio. You and I have nothing in common, nothing on which to base a good relationship. Anything between us would be over in a flash.'

'I generally find that I can maintain my performance for little longer than a "flash",' he purred and she gave a murmur of exasperation.

'Alessio, please.' For some reason it suddenly seemed desperate that she make him understand. 'I will not allow myself to make huge decisions based on something as fleeting as chemistry.'

'It wouldn't be fleeting.' Dark lashes shielded his gaze. 'I'd want you again and again, in every conceivable position.'

Her limbs weak and her heart pounding, Lindsay stood up and dropped her napkin on the table. Why had she ever thought she could beat him at his own game? 'Sex without love is an extremely unsatisfying form of entertainment. I'm not interested.'

'I've never left a woman unsatisfied in my life.'

'All right, you win.' She lifted a hand in a gesture of supplication, so desperately unsettled by their verbal exchange that she knew she needed to escape. 'Enough. I don't want to talk about it anymore. I'm here in place of my sister. If you want me to do any legal work for you, then please knock on my door.'

And, please, don't let it be any time soon.

CHAPTER SIX

LINDSAY stood under the shower, letting the jets of ice-cold water cool her thoroughly overheated body.

Why, oh, why had she thought she'd be able to cope with being alone with Alessio for a week? After barely a few hours in his company she was so tense and wound up that she felt physically sick.

Her body was tormented by a nagging sensation that no amount of cold water could cure. He hadn't even touched her and yet she felt weak and limp and just utterly *drugged* with longing for something that she absolutely shouldn't and couldn't have.

Angry with herself, she thrust the palm of her hand against the shower knob and the flow of water ceased.

Alessio Capelli was arrogant, cold and frighteningly unemotional. Presumably those traits had contributed to his success in his chosen career. How else would he have been able to destroy people's marriages without losing sleep?

But the problem wasn't him, was it? The real problem was *her*. Her feelings; her response to him—

Feeling despair seep into every pore of her body, Lindsay sank onto the floor of the shower and wrapped her arms around her knees. Her hair hung wet down her back and she swept a hand over her face to clear the water from her eyelashes. Yes, he was arrogant, cold and frighteningly unemotional, but what really bothered her was the fact that everything he'd said to her had been correct.

No matter how much she'd tried to focus her mind on something else, she *had* found herself thinking of nothing but sex. One glance at his firm mouth and she'd started wondering how he kissed; a chance glimpse of dark male hair at the neck of his shirt and she'd immediately imagined him naked.

With a murmur of self-disgust, she covered her face with her hands.

She couldn't stop imagining the two of them together and for the first time in her life she was starting to understand how sheer sexual hunger could be so overwhelming that it could drive a person to make *really* bad decisions.

If he were here now, she'd be touching him.

And that would have been a disaster because Alessio Capelli was *totally* wrong for her.

Yes, he would undoubtedly be a skilled and exciting lover, but what else would he give her? The answer to that was *nothing but trouble*.

With a low groan she let her hands drop into her lap and leaned her head back against the wall. It would have been so easy to just knock on the door of his villa and let him take it from there. And she had no doubt that he would have instantly taken control. He was that sort of man, wasn't he?

And then what?

She was only too aware of the dangers of that sort of relationship. She spent her working life counselling people to look deeper.

So why was she struggling with her decision?

Because never in her life before had she wanted a man the way she wanted Alessio Capelli.

Suddenly she felt a burst of uncharacteristic anger towards Ruby. This was her fault. If she hadn't abandoned her job…

Was Ruby experiencing a similar degree of chemistry with Dino Capelli? If so, then it was little wonder she'd vanished without caring about her job or her sister.

And anyway, how could she be angry with Ruby? It wasn't really her sister's fault, was it?

After her uncertain, disordered childhood and then the collapse of a disastrous relationship, it was easy to see how she'd been dazzled by the wealth and charisma of the Capelli brothers.

With a sigh, Lindsay got to her feet and wrapped herself in one of the huge soft towels that were left ready for her use.

It was time to pull herself together. What use would she be to Ruby if she was suffering from a bruised heart herself?

No, sex with Alessio Capelli would undoubtedly have been amazing, but it was too high a price to pay for the mess she'd be in afterwards.

She was glad she'd walked away. In fact she was proud of herself.

Lindsay dried her hair methodically and then slid into a sheer silk nightdress that was nothing like her normal choice of bed wear.

But as she slipped into the large canopied bed she felt suddenly more alone than she'd ever felt in her life.

Without doubt she was the only woman who had ever walked away from him.

Trying to dismiss images of a powerful arrogant Italian stretched out next to her, she pressed her face into the pillows and pulled the soft cover over her shoulders.

Instead of focusing on the nagging throb low in her body, she needed to think of his bad points. Of all the logical reasons why they shouldn't be together.

And there were certainly plenty to choose from.

Tired after a sleepless night, Lindsay forced her trembling legs along the smooth stone path that led to the Beach Club.

Given the choice she would have eaten breakfast alone.

She would have locked the door and stayed indoors in the air-conditioned tranquillity of her luxurious villa, but that wasn't an option. She was here to do a job and she was well aware that if she didn't play the part, then Alessio might still fire Ruby.

At least now she was on her guard. She'd let herself become complacent. She'd *totally* underestimated the devastating effect he had on her.

But now she was prepared.

Having been awake for most of the night, she'd had more than enough time to select her outfit for the day, and this time she'd been less cavalier in her choice of dress.

She'd bypassed swimming costumes, shorts and sarongs and instead chosen a white skirt that drifted down to mid-thigh. She'd teamed it with a strap top in a pale shade of lilac, cut high enough on her chest to ensure that no cleavage was revealed. And it fitted perfectly. She was confident that there was no chance that it would gape or reveal anything if she leaned forward. In an impulse of femininity that she didn't want to examine too closely, she'd slipped some delicate silver bangles onto her arm.

It was fine.

Everything was fine.

And everything remained fine until she walked onto the terrace and saw him.

He was seated at a table next to the beautiful swimming pool, a cup of coffee half drunk on the table in front of him.

Every part of his masculine physique emanating power and authority, he was talking to a man in a lightweight suit, but the moment he saw Lindsay his eyes narrowed and he said something that Lindsay couldn't hear.

The other man melted swiftly into the background leaving Lindsay the entire focus of Alessio's attention.

'*Buon giorno.*' He spoke in a low tone that was inaudible to all around, his eyes cool and assessing. 'Did you sleep well?'

'Perfectly, thank you.' She pulled out a chair and sat down opposite him, ignoring his knowing smile. 'Any sign of your client?'

Please say yes, she begged silently. A third person might dilute the tension that seemed to surround them.

'There's been a hurricane warning. He's decided not to fly out until the weather improves.'

Startled, she looked at him. 'A hurricane?'

'Don't worry. Kingfisher Cay hasn't suffered a direct hit once in the past sixty years. It will pass us by.'

Lindsay glanced up at the blue sky, noticing a few wisps of cloud on the horizon. 'Let's hope you're right.'

'Are you afraid of storms?'

'I love storms—' without looking at him, she helped herself to slices of fresh pineapple and mango from a plate in the centre of the table '—so if you're hoping that I'll seek the shelter of your strong arms, you're going to be disappointed.'

Alessio laughed. 'So far I haven't had to rely on the weather to entice a woman into my bed.'

'I'm sure you haven't.' She made a point of examining the deep gold flesh of the mango. 'Where there's money, there will always be women.'

'Ouch, Lindsay, that was cruel.' He was still laughing at her, apparently totally unaffected by her dig.

'No, really—I feel sorry for you—' picking up a fork, she speared a piece of mango '—you must be incredibly lonely. Meaningless sex has to become boring after a while.'

'Obviously you've never had really good sex,' he said dryly and Lindsay concentrated on her plate, taking her time over selecting her next piece of tropical fruit.

'For you it's a sort of sport, isn't it? A type of physical workout. You just don't engage your emotions. Don't you want *more*?'

'"More" being marriage?' He drained his coffee. 'I think you know me better than that.'

'I don't know you at all.'

'That's your choice,' he said silkily, his dark eyes glinting dangerously as he watched her. 'Feel free to take a voyage of discovery at your convenience. You look tired, Lindsay. Did something keep you awake last night? Your thoughts, perhaps?'

'I slept perfectly,' she lied. 'So if you have no client to see today, what are you going to do?'

'I have another difficult case that needs my attention. I intend to go out on the yacht. A change of scene sometimes helps me focus.'

Weak with relief at the news that he wasn't going to be around during the day, Lindsay finished the fruit on her plate and actually managed a smile. 'Of course. Don't worry about me. I quite understand that you need some time to yourself.' Maybe this wasn't going to be so hard after all. She could curl up in her villa with a book. Once she was confident he was nowhere near the island, she might even change into one of those revealing swimming costumes and risk a swim in the sea. 'I'll be fine.'

'I know you'll be fine—' he reached out a hand and helped himself to a piece of exotic fruit from the platter in front of him '—because you'll be with me. You're my assistant, remember? Where I go, you go.'

'When you're working, yes. But if you're simply having a day off on your yacht—'

'I don't take days off. I'll simply be working in a different venue.' His strong fingers dissected the fruit with ruthless precision while Lindsay stared in dismay.

He expected her to go with him? 'You'll be working on a boat?'

'A catamaran, to be precise. She's moored over there on the jetty.'

Lindsay turned her head and stared at the beautiful craft, the hull glistening white in the dazzling Caribbean sunshine. Just the two of them. Trapped. *On that?* Being on an island was bad enough, but being on a boat— 'I know absolutely nothing about boats.'

'I'll handle the boat.' He nodded to one of the waiters who instantly produced more coffee. 'Your duties will involve something else entirely.'

Her stomach lurched. 'What exactly will you want me to do?'

'I'm not sure yet.' He gave a slow smile. 'But when I've decided, you'll be the first to know.'

Despite her reservations, the sail was exhilarating—two hours of glorious sunshine while the boat skimmed joyously across the water, the sails arching against the kiss of the wind.

By the time Alessio finally sailed the boat into a curved, sheltered bay, Lindsay's face was pink from the sun and stinging with the spray of the sea.

And she felt fantastic. Unable to hide her elation, she kneeled on the seat and peered over the side of the catamaran, down into the clear depths of the blue Caribbean sea. It was like looking into an aquarium. The sun sparkled on the water and tropical fish in a rainbow of colours darted beneath her. And ahead of her was a perfect curve of white sand, fringed by palm trees and surprisingly lush vegetation.

She glanced back at him. 'Are we the only people here?'

'You wanted a party?' His movements sure and confident, he secured a rope and lowered the anchor.

'It's like being shipwrecked,' Lindsay murmured, turning her head and staring at the stretch of deserted beach.

'Five-star shipwreck.' Alessio produced a bottle of chilled champagne and deftly removed the cork. Pouring the bubbling liquid into two thin-stemmed flutes, he held one out to her. 'To a productive afternoon.'

Lindsay rose slowly to her feet and took the glass hesitantly. 'I don't drink in the middle of the day.'

'Take a sip.' Alessio raised his own glass in her direction. 'I think you might be about to discover a whole new vice.'

Because of the way he was looking at her, *because of the way he was making her feel*, Lindsay took a tentative sip and the surprisingly light and delicious drink seemed to sparkle in her mouth. She swallowed and smiled. 'It's delicious,' she admitted and took another sip. 'Really refreshing. It doesn't taste alcoholic.'

'Well, believe me, it is.' Putting down his own glass, he leaned behind her and carefully coiled a rope. 'Don't drink too much, especially if you're not used to it. Boats and alcohol don't mix and I don't want to be fishing you out of the water.'

'Then why did you want me to drink it?'

'Because this particular champagne is an experience that everyone should try at least once in their lives.' He gave a slow smile. 'A bit like no-strings sex.'

She took another sip of the delicious champagne, watching as the sun glinted on his glossy hair. 'For me, sex has to be an expression of love.'

'That's because you haven't tried the other sort.'

'I wouldn't want to.'

He turned to face her, a smile softening the hard lines of his mouth. 'Oh, you do want to, *tesoro*.' His voice soft, he stepped forward so that his body was virtually touching hers. 'You do want to. But you're afraid.'

Suddenly dizzy, she put her glass down on the seat next to her. 'Of course I'm afraid. I'm afraid of being hurt.'

'No, that isn't it.' He leaned closer to her and she felt the roughness of his jaw graze the softness of her cheek as he whispered in her ear. 'I think you're afraid that you might actually enjoy it. And then where would you be? A relation-ship counsellor who has made her name dismissing casual sex, suddenly embroiled in a no-strings affair. You'd have to rethink your career.'

Her eyes closed. He smelt fantastic and her senses swirled dangerously, sucking her down. Telling herself that it was just the champagne, she stepped backwards and would have fallen over the coiled rope if he hadn't reached out and steadied her.

Instinctively she put a hand on his shoulder, feeling rock-hard muscle under her fingers. *He's strong*, she thought dizzily—*really strong*.

For a moment she just stood there, her body sending out signals that she was desperate to ignore.

Then, without warning, he released her. 'Are you wearing a swimming costume under that outfit?'

'Yes.' Her mouth was dry, her heart thumping and her mind—her mind was in a mess.

'Then I suggest that a dip in cold water might do us both good.' Without waiting for her response, he stripped off his shirt and shorts, poised for a moment on the edge of the boat before executing a perfect dive into the sun-dappled water.

Suddenly dizzy, Lindsay realised that it had actually been quite a while since she'd taken a breath. To be precise, since the moment he'd stripped off his shirt exposing powerful shoulders and bronzed skin.

No wonder women chased him, she thought weakly, watching as he emerged from the depths of the water, the water streaming from his dark hair as he wiped a hand over his face to clear his vision.

'Come on, Lindsay.'

She looked at him with something close to desperation. Joining him in the water somehow seemed symbolic. If she jumped—if she made that leap— 'The boat might drift.'

'The boat is fine. If you don't come in, I'll come and get you.'

Slowly, she wriggled out of her shorts and tee shirt. It *was* hot, she told herself, and her costume was perfectly decent. It didn't enter her head to follow him into the water head-first. Instead she walked to the end of the boat and gingerly picked her way down the ladder, holding tightly, pausing slightly as she registered the depth of the water beneath her.

'Typical Lindsay,' Alessio drawled, 'never one to jump if she can hold on to a ladder.'

Ignoring the amusement in his tone, she forced herself to let go of the ladder.

The cool, smooth water closed over her heated body and for a moment she felt small and insignificant, with nothing but ocean beneath and around her.

'This feels a bit weird.' Disconcerted, she glanced down and gasped as a shoal of blue fish darted beneath them. 'Oh, my goodness—'

'Blue Tang. The diving in this area is spectacular.'

Feeling a bit foolish, she swam a little closer to him. 'Are there sharks?'

His eyes focused on something over her shoulder and the laughter faded from his face. 'Ah—it seems that there are,' he said softly. 'Don't move, Lindsay, he's probably just being nosy—'

With a horrified gasp, she clutched at his shoulders and, too late, saw the wicked gleam in his eyes. 'Oh—I hate you. *I hate you!* That was an awful thing to do.'

'There are no sharks.' His hand curved around her waist. 'The reef stops them swimming this close to the land.'

'It does feel slightly menacing, having all that water beneath you,' she confessed, not brushing his hand away quite so quickly as she would have done had they been on dry land. 'It's beautiful. And—weird,' she admitted, 'not being able to touch the bottom.'

'You haven't swum off a boat before?'

'I don't generally find the opportunity during my working day.'

He gave a slow smile. 'You need to rethink your working day, *tesoro*. Life is to be lived, not just survived.' His hand was still on her back—large, warm, *strong*.

'I like my life.'

'That's because you don't know what you're missing. Stay there, I'll fetch you a snorkel.' He swam away from her, hauled himself back onto the boat with athletic ease and returned moments later with two masks in his hand. 'Try this.' Ignoring her protests, he adjusted the mask and eased it over her head. 'Put your head in the water and see if it leaks.'

After a moment of hesitation she decided that it would be safer just to follow his orders for once, and dutifully held her breath and put her face in the water.

An amazingly beautiful and varied underwater world stretched out beneath her and when she finally had to lift her head to breathe, she was smiling. 'All right. Just this once I'm willing to concede that you're right about something. I love it.'

He showed her how to breathe through the tube and how to dive down and clear it. Then he swam off and left her to get used to it by herself.

She experimented, becoming more and more adventurous and delighted by the brightly coloured fish she saw darting in shoals beneath her. When she finally stopped swimming and lifted her head, she saw Alessio taking the boat onto the beach.

She swam to the shore, removed her mask and snorkel and walked towards him. The white sand was silky soft under her feet, the sun blazing down on her head and shoulders.

'I've packed us some provisions.' He hauled some baskets out of the boat and handed her one. 'This island is very pretty. Worth exploring.' He dragged the boat farther up the beach, away from the lick of the sea.

Then he pulled out a cool box and a rug and strolled farther up the beach towards the palm trees. 'Your pale English skin will need the shade.'

Unlike him, she thought ruefully, scanning his golden brown shoulders and bronzed back as he casually threw the rug onto the sand. He had the sort of skin that turned brown in an instant.

He lay on his back on the rug and closed his eyes. 'An hour,' he murmured. 'We'll spend an hour here and then we'll sail back to Kingfisher Cay.'

She sat down, leaving a respectable distance between the two of them. 'How did you find this place?'

'I was sailing one day and came across it. I bought it.'

'Retail therapy, Alessio?'

Eyes still closed, he smiled. 'I had a wild idea that I might build a villa for myself on it one day. I like the fact that it's relatively inaccessible. The way the land curves means that it isn't visible from any other island. No photographers with long lenses. I like my privacy.'

'Is that why you don't allow cameras on Kingfisher Cay?'

'Yes. I want the guests to know that they're truly on holiday.'

'So are you going to build yourself a house here?'

'Maybe. At the moment we only use it for privileged guests who want a deserted island experience.'

'How did you find Kingfisher Cay?' Suddenly curious, she frowned down at him. 'I mean, you're Italian.'

'Sicilian.' His tone a shade cooler, he raised himself up on his elbows. 'I'm Sicilian.'

And he looks Sicilian, she thought desperately, *with those strands of blue-black hair flopping over his bronzed forehead.* He looked dark and dangerous and— 'All right, you're Sicilian—' she spoke quickly '—but why the Caribbean? You have your own islands in Italy.'

'No one would sell me Sicily.' His eyes gleamed with sardonic humour and she found herself laughing too, although a tiny part of her wondered whether perhaps he wasn't joking.

'Do you have to *own* everything?'

'If you're asking if I'm a possessive man—' he gave a slow, expressive shrug of his broad shoulders '*Sì*. If I want something, then, yes, I have to own it.' His eyes lingered on her face and she shivered, suddenly agonisingly aware that it was just the two of them on a deserted island.

'Can I ask you something else?'

'Ask.'

'Who was it that put you off marriage?'

For a moment he didn't respond and then he sat up, the muscles in his abdomen tensing as he leaned forward and flipped open the lid of an elegant basket. 'Are you hungry?'

That was it? He was going to ignore her question? 'You said I could ask you something—'

'And you did.' Reaching into the basket, he removed a number of dishes that wouldn't have disgraced a top restaurant.

'But you haven't answered me.'

'I didn't say that I'd answer.' He broke the bread in half and handed her a piece. 'I said you could ask.'

Exasperated, she looked at him. 'Do you ever stop being a lawyer?'

'Am I being a lawyer?'

'You guard every word you say.'

His eyes lingered on her face for a moment and then he smiled. 'In much the same way that you guard everything you do.'

She pulled at the bread with her fingers. 'You should have been a politician. You only ever reveal what you want to reveal. Doesn't matter what the question is, because the only answer you're going to get from Alessio Capelli is the one he wants to give.'

'Spilling my guts has never been my style.'

'And yet you have a really high profile in the press.'

'Their choice, not mine.' He was totally indifferent. 'I give them nothing.'

'Why don't you live in Sicily? Or aren't you prepared to discuss that either?'

'Sicily isn't a good base for an international business. I divide my time between my office in New York and my office in Rome.'

Lindsay finished eating and wiped her fingers. 'Do you ever go back to Sicily? Do you have family there?'

There was an imperceptible change in him. 'Just my brother. And he's with me in Rome.'

'Are your parents alive?'

He moved so swiftly that she didn't stand a chance. One moment she was sitting on the sand, congratulating herself that they were actually managing to sustain a conversation about something other than sex or divorce—*a faltering, fragile conversation maybe, but a conversation neverthe-less*—and the next, she was on her back in the sand and his hard, powerful body was pressing down on hers.

'I don't give interviews, *tesoro*.' For a few suspended seconds his mouth hovered tantalisingly close, almost but not quite touching her. And the promise of that touch made her lips tingle and her body ache, and the stab of delicious anticipation was so agonising that she could hardly breathe as she waited for him to kiss her. Her senses were primed, her pulse rate frantic, her nerve endings exploding like fireworks on bonfire night. And just when she'd decided that he wasn't going to do it—*that it wasn't going to happen*—he did.

And it was nothing like she'd imagined it to be.

Alessio Capelli was pure alpha male—arrogant, confident, imposing his will on those around him.

Whenever she'd thought about kissing him, she'd imagined his hand in her hair, his mouth rough and demand-ing as he took what he wanted. So the slow, seductive pressure of his mouth on hers came as a shock. He was a skilled, expert kisser—a man who knew exactly how to draw the maximum response from a woman. The heat rushed through her body, lighting every nerve ending like a match held against paper. And she melted in the heat of that kiss, her body growing warm and heavy as sizzling excitement concentrated itself low in her pelvis.

With slow, deliberate precision, he coaxed her lips apart and she felt the intimate stroke of his tongue stealing both her breath and her willpower. And she didn't ever want him to stop because it was the most delicious, perfect kiss she could have imagined and if the world had ended right then she wouldn't have cared.

It was as if he'd drugged her, his touch sending every rational thought from her spinning brain.

His body shifted above her and she felt his warm, strong hand slide across her shoulder. She was held immobile by sensual bondage; it was only when his lips moved from her mouth to her breast that she realised he'd somehow removed the strap of her swimsuit.

Control slid away from her and she moaned and lifted herself against the warmth of his mouth, desperate for his touch. Her frantic response obviously met with his approval because he gave a soft, appreciative laugh.

'*Adoro il tuo corpo.*' His voice husky, he concentrated his attention on one dusky pink nipple. 'I love your body.' As if to prove just how much he loved her body, his hand slid slowly down her thigh, the touch of his fingers creating havoc with her senses.

It was exciting, terrifying and utterly, utterly addictive.

Desperately she tried to regain some control over what was happening, but every time she tried to gasp out a protest he'd touch her in a particular way and she'd be sucked back down into a whirlpool of wicked, delicious pleasure from which there was no escape.

It was the heavy thrust of his erection against her thigh that finally shocked her out of her state of dizzy stupor.

'No—Alessio, no—' With a groan of denial, she put her hand on his chest, resisting the impulse to stroke rather than stop. But she had to stop. 'I can't—not like this—'

He was above her, his weight pressing her into the soft sand, powerfully male and unashamedly aroused. 'What's wrong with this? I am too heavy for you?' Suddenly he sounded impossibly Italian, his normally confident English slightly less fluent than usual. Slowly, he trailed a gentle, exploratory finger over her mouth. 'You are feeling shy?'

There was no way she could put into words what she was feeling because she'd never felt it before. She was used to being in control. Normally she thought of herself as assertive and self-reliant, but where were those qualities now? She was lying passive, dominated by a sexually confident male, and that was bad enough, but the thing that really shamed her was that she was enjoying it. A small secret part of her was thrilled by his strength and virility.

Alessio Capelli had never heard the phrase 'politically correct', she thought dizzily, closing her eyes to break the sizzling connection between them. 'We haven't—this is just impulse and it's all wrong. Sex should be a conscious decision, not an impulse. It should be planned.' *Oh, Lindsay, Lindsay, you really shouldn't be doing this. If you eat too much chocolate you put on weight, and if you sleep with men like Alessio Capelli—*

'So far, this is going exactly the way I planned, *tesoro*,' he murmured, amusement in his voice as he lowered his dark head and delivered a lingering kiss to her neck. 'Tell me something, Lindsay—' his voice was a soft, dangerous purr '—if there was no tomorrow, would you do this?'

He dangled temptation in front of her without hesitation

or conscience and she gave a low moan, rejecting the answer that came into her head.

'There *is* a tomorrow.'

'But sometimes it is good to live your life as though there isn't,' he murmured, his fingers gently tracing her cheek. 'That is good, no?'

For a moment Lindsay lay there dazed and then gradually his words sank into her brain. 'Wait a minute.' Her voice was husky and she cleared her throat. 'Did you just say that you planned this?'

'We're alone and half-naked on a desert island, *tesoro*.' His mouth discovered a sensitive spot just under her jawbone and Lindsay's insides clenched.

'And that makes sex inevitable?'

'I hate to let an opportunity go to waste,' he breathed softly and she closed her eyes tightly because the shift from meltdown to misery had happened in the space of a heartbeat.

Dear God, she was a fool.

'I'm a person, Alessio, not an opportunity.' Her voice breaking slightly, she pushed at his chest and he shifted away from her, his dark eyes narrowed in question.

'You appeared to be enjoying yourself.'

'I enjoy chocolate—but I know when to say no. Don't you have any morals?'

'Obviously I do.' His tone cool, Alessio rolled onto his back. 'You said no. I stopped.'

'Do us both a favour next time—don't start.' Her body felt warm and alive, as if someone had flicked a switch that could never again be turned off. 'Don't touch me again, Alessio.'

'*Sì*, you are right—it was good.' He gave a low laugh and she looked at him fiercely.

'I didn't say it was good—'

'But you don't want me to touch you again—' his eyes

drifted shut, the smile on his hard mouth one of raw male arrogance '—and that says everything there is to be said.'

'It says, I don't want you to touch me again!' Her heart was pumping like an athlete in a sprint. 'Are you having trouble with your English?'

'No, but I think you're having trouble with your "choices",' he said silkily. 'You were sure what you wanted—now, you're not so sure.'

She scrambled to her feet, averting her eyes from the haze of dark hair on his bronzed chest. 'I want to go back to Kingfisher Cay. I want to go back right now.' Before she did something, really, *really* foolish.

'Unfortunately, we can't do that.'

'Yes, we can.' Control was slipping through her fingers. 'You sailed here, you can sail back again.'

'No, I can't.' His tone was suddenly serious. 'You and I have a real problem, Lindsay.'

She lifted her fingers to her forehead, anger fading to despair. 'I know we have a problem.' Her body was still humming with sexual awareness, but she took a deep breath and looked him in the eye. 'It will be fine if we just ignore it. We're both adults and we're perfectly capable of resisting temptation if we choose to do so.'

'We're at cross purposes. I wasn't talking about the chemistry between us. I don't see *that* as a problem.' He turned, a sardonic smile on his face. 'And just so that we're both clear, I have no intention of resisting temptation, so, if that's the route you plan to take, you're on your own. You'll be resisting without my help.'

Still trying to cope with his cool admission that he had no intention of resisting temptation, Lindsay bit her lip. 'Well, if that's not the problem—'

'When did you last look at the sea or the sky, Lindsay?'

His tone deceptively gentle, his eyes flickered behind her. 'Do you remember that storm I mentioned?'

Storm? For a moment she stared at him, her mind refusing to go further back than the kiss.

And then she turned her head and looked at the ocean.

Somehow, at some point during their picnic—and afterwards—the sea had turned from glasslike smooth stillness, to an angry, boiling furnace. Waves lashed the shore and the sky had turned from perfect blue to ominous grey. 'Oh, my goodness—I didn't notice—'

'I think we were both rather distracted,' he drawled, irony in his gaze as he sprang to his feet.

Lindsay felt a flash of panic. 'Call someone. Use your mobile phone.'

'I didn't bring it. There's no signal here. And anyway, no boats will come out in this and the wind is too strong for the seaplane. We'll have to wait it out.'

Lindsay's insides lurched. 'Is it the hurricane?'

'No, but I suspect it must have changed course or we wouldn't be experiencing this weather.' His gaze lingered on the sky for a moment and then he bent down and gathered up their things. 'I'll just secure the boat and then we'll go and find shelter. There's an old abandoned cottage on the other side of the island. It will be more protected there. We'll shelter until the storm passes.'

Horrified, she stared at him. 'And how long will that be?'

'I have absolutely no idea.'

'You're suggesting that we stay here alone?' She licked her lips and her eyes slid to the angry sea. 'You did this on purpose.'

'I'm flattered by your assessment of my powers,' he said dryly, 'but even I can't change the course of a hurricane. With luck it will just graze the island and lose power over the sea. Come on. If it doesn't blow itself out, you'll have plenty of time to blame me for the sins of the world over the next few days. Pick up the picnic blanket and the rest of the food. I need to see to the boat.'

'But it's already on the beach—'

'Trust me, in a few hours, this won't be beach.'

And they were going to be trapped together. She looked at him in horror, expecting to see signs of worry on his face, but his eyes gleamed with something that looked like anticipation. 'You're actually enjoying this, aren't you?'

'It's something out of the ordinary and, yes, that's exciting in its own way. Unlike you, I don't like life to be too pre-dictable. Where's the challenge in that? Come on. We need to find ourselves some shelter.'

CHAPTER SEVEN

'YOU'RE shivering. Are you cold?' His tone sharp, Alessio hauled the rest of their things into the single-storey cottage and immediately the sound of the building wind was muffled.

'I'm not cold,' Lindsay lied, resisting the temptation to rub her hands down her bare arms. Why, oh, why was fate so cruel? Why couldn't she at least have had something with her that could have covered her up? She wished now that she'd returned to the boat to pick up more provisions, but Alessio had insisted that they move as fast as possible.

And it had been the right decision. By the time they'd walked for twenty minutes along the beach, the wind had risen dramatically.

She'd been relieved when she'd spotted the cottage on the far side of the tiny island. It was slightly protected by the curve of the land and Lindsay could see that they'd be safer there than in the little bay where they'd landed.

'What is this place?' The cottage was obviously old and she hesitated on the doorstep, wary of trespassing. 'Who owns it?'

'I suppose I do, technically. Before me it belonged to an eccentric millionaire who didn't much like people.' Alessio was prowling around the deserted rooms, as if he were looking for something. Occasionally he'd pause and put his hand against a window. 'We'll shelter in here. Stay away from the window in case the glass is blown in. We have rugs, plenty of water and some food. We'll be fine for a few days, if necessary.'

'A few *days*?' Appalled, Lindsay gaped at him. 'I can't stay here for a few days! I need to contact Ruby.'

He spread the rug on the floor. 'It doesn't make much difference whether you're on Kingfisher Cay, or here. Ruby isn't answering your calls.'

'But what if she tries to contact me?' Lindsay paced the floor, desperately worried. 'What if she rings in a panic? What if she needs my advice? I won't be answering my phone and *what will she do then*?'

'She might have to make a decision on her own. Believe me, that would do her the world of good.' Watching her pace the room, he frowned suddenly. 'You're stranded in a storm and still you're thinking about your sister. When exactly do you worry about yourself? You should be asking me if we're going to get out of here, or if the cottage is likely to be blown away.'

'We'll be fine, I'm sure.' Barely registering those possibilities, Lindsay started to bite one of her nails and then let her hand drop. 'But if Ruby needs to contact me—what if she hears about this storm?'

'She doesn't know you're with me, so she won't understand its relevance. And anyway, you're safe here.'

Suddenly realising just how isolated they were, Lindsay felt her stomach flip. She didn't feel safe. She didn't feel safe at all, and her growing tension had nothing to do with the threatening weather. Outside, the wind was starting to whistle and howl, buffeting the cottage and rattling the windows. But the real threat to her well-being was on the inside.

Dressed only in his swimming shorts, Alessio was now sprawled on the rug watching her.

'Are you going to pace all night?'

'I can't relax—'

'When are you going to let your sister lead her own life?

You try and control her every movement—it's no wonder she's rebelled and vanished into the sunset. You created this situation by behaving more like a mother than a sister.'

It was as if he'd punched her.

Appalled, Lindsay stared at him. 'No.' She shook her head in furious denial. 'I *don't* control her. I just offer her support.'

'Support is "I'm here if you need me",' Alessio drawled. 'Support isn't "you're not doing what I think you should do".'

Lindsay's head was filled with images of a vulnerable toddler clinging to her in bed, night after night. 'You don't understand—'

'*Maledizione*, why do you think she hasn't called?' His tone was brutally direct. 'Because she knows you're going to disapprove of what she's doing. She knows that when you pick up that phone, all she's going to get from you is a lecture.'

'No.' Lindsay's lips felt dry. 'No, that isn't—'

'Have you ever tried to understand her? Did you ever ask yourself why she wanted to stay in Rome? I'll tell you why—because it was the only way she could possibly run her life without your constant interference.'

Frozen to the spot, Lindsay could barely breathe. 'That isn't true.' Her stomach heaved and for a moment she actually felt physically sick. 'And you have no right to say those things to me. What does someone like you know about love? Or relationships?'

She turned and paced back across the room, her arms wrapped around her body as she struggled to hold herself together.

It wasn't true. None of the horrid things he was saying was true.

Yes, she was protective of Ruby. But she was the older sister. It was her responsibility to look after Ruby. She'd always done it, ever since they were children.

'Will you let me sleep in your bed, Linny?'

She'd smothered Ruby with love, compensating for the

lack of care and affection they'd received from their parents. She'd been the sister *and* the mother.

Lindsay dug her hands into her hair as she forced herself to examine the facts.

Of course she was going to support her sister and offer advice. She'd been the very best sister she could be. Hadn't she?

Tormented by a tiny seed of doubt, Lindsay felt as though her entire world were unravelling.

She'd been so sure of herself. So certain. And suddenly she just didn't feel certain anymore.

She needed space to think—

She needed to get out of this confined space—

Somehow she managed to make her lips move. 'I need some air.' Tugging open the door, she staggered as a powerful gust almost dragged it out of her hand, the wind howling like a choir of a thousand ghosts, daring her to venture outside.

But Lindsay didn't care—

Whatever lay outside, it had to be better than being trapped with Alessio.

Wincing as the door was almost taken off its hinges, Alessio spent a few seconds cursing the whole female race and their tendency to the dramatic, before springing to his feet.

Hurricane-force winds were blowing outside and she'd decided that she *needed some air*?

Was she crazy?

But even as he asked himself that question, something slightly uncomfortable twisted inside him. No, she wasn't crazy. She was just upset. Very, very upset.

And he was the cause of that upset.

Unaccustomed to experiencing feelings of guilt, Alessio strode towards the door, reminding himself that he'd merely told her the truth. And if it had been a painful truth, well, that was because she'd been deluding herself.

In the long term, he'd done her a favour.

She'd probably thank him.

So why was he wishing he could wind the clock back and been given an opportunity to keep his mouth shut?

Trying to dismiss the image of her white face and the distressed look in her eyes, Alessio strode to the door.

If she didn't have the sense to know it was dangerous out there, then he was going to have to go and fetch her.

Immediately the strength of the wind stole the breath from his lungs and he wondered how someone as slight as Lindsay had managed to stay upright in the path of such a powerful force.

As he secured the door behind him he found himself wondering why she hadn't turned back.

But he knew the answer to that. She hadn't turned back because of him. She was either so angry with him she couldn't bear to be within the same four walls, or else she was so upset by what he'd said that she needed to think.

Either way, she was putting herself in physical danger.

Black, deadly clouds had replaced perfect blue sky and Alessio glanced along the beach, searching for a solitary figure.

And then he saw her. Her arms were wrapped around her body and she was staring out to sea, apparently oblivious to the anger of the storm that was building. Her pale hair had broken loose from the clasp and for once she hadn't bothered to pin it up again. As if to taunt her with that fact, the wind caught it and blew it wildly around her face and shoulders. She looked like a mermaid, contemplating a return to the sea. She also looked—fragile.

Alessio frowned. *Fragile?* He always thought of Lindsay Lockheart as composed and controlled. Even the night she'd been attacked on the streets of Rome, she'd been remarkably collected, more concerned about her sister than herself.

But she didn't look composed or controlled. She looked—broken.

Swearing fluently in two different languages, he strode across to her, ready to blast her for taking such a stupid risk.

But as he drew closer he saw that her cheeks were wet and her eyes were glistening.

Maledizione—

Alessio executed an emergency stop, his natural inclination to retreat in the face of female emotion acting as a break. Given the choice, he would have preferred to do battle with ten storms than mop up tears.

He took a step backwards.

Obviously she wanted to be alone, he reasoned. If she'd wanted his company, she would have stayed in the cottage.

Convincing himself that what she needed most was some space and time to herself—*after all, hadn't she chosen to come out here alone?*—he was about to retreat when another powerful gust of wind slammed into them and she lost her balance.

In one stride, Alessio was next to her. He closed his arms around her and braced his strong legs to support them both against the force of the wind. 'Do you have a death wish? It isn't safe out here!' She felt impossibly fragile and he wondered why she hadn't already been blown over.

He glared down at her, but his feelings of anger and exasperation dissolved in an instant as he registered her tortured expression. '*Why* are you looking at me like that?'

This was a different Lindsay. A desperately unsure, insecure Lindsay. There was no sign of the competent exterior that she presented to the world. She even *looked* different, for once oblivious to the fact that her hair was blowing loose around her face and the fact that she was dressed only in a swimming costume. She looked incredibly young.

Incredibly beautiful...

Engulfed by a sudden explosion of lust that was almost more powerful than the storm, Alessio contemplated slinging her over his shoulder and taking her back to the cottage for the type of one-on-one comfort he knew he was capable of delivering.

He was responsible for her upset and he was confident that he could fix it.

But then she lifted her eyes to his and she looked so vulnerable that for once he decided not to say what was on his mind.

Instead he dragged his gaze from the trembling curve of her soft mouth and tried to focus on something non sexual. *Like the fact that they were both about to be blown to the outer reaches of the Caribbean.* Torn between concern for her safety and guilt that he was the cause of her distress, he tried to haul her back up the path, but she refused to move. 'We have to go inside.'

She looked at him blankly and exasperation mingled with concern because she was the most decisive woman he'd ever met and yet she was clearly incapable of making any sort of decision.

Tears glistened on her lashes and shadows flickered across her eyes. 'What if you're right?' She had to raise her voice to be heard above the howl of the wind and he gritted his teeth.

There was a storm blowing and she wanted to *talk*?

'I *am* right,' Alessio assured her, confident that it was the right response regardless of the question. He slid his arm around her shoulders and urged her up the path. 'We need to get inside. Now. *Pronto.* Before we find ourselves transported to the next island.'

'No. I mean about Ruby.' She stopped, her hand in her hair to prevent it from blowing wildly around her face. 'What if you're right about Ruby? What if the reason Ruby isn't ringing me is because she thinks I'll judge her? What if it is my fault? What if I've driven her away?' Another powerful gust of wind almost knocked her off her feet and Alessio made a unilateral decision and scooped her into his arms.

She'll thank me later, he thought as he strode back up the narrow, sandy path to the comparative safety of the cottage. Shouldering the door shut against the raging, angry storm, he lowered her gently to the floor.

'*Don't* leave the cottage again.' His tone was sharper than he'd intended and when he saw the sheen in her eyes he cursed himself for not being more sympathetic. If he didn't tread carefully she was going to dissolve in a sodden heap and that was the last thing he wanted or needed.

Resigned to the inevitable, he waited for her to collapse sobbing against his chest, but instead she turned away.

'Just give me a minute.'

On unfamiliar territory, Alessio stared at her rigid shoulders, trying to work out what he was supposed to do next. Although he had plentiful experience of tearful women, he'd never been with one who didn't want him to see her crying. And everything about her body language told him that Lindsay Lockheart was trying very hard not to let him see her crying.

Alessio hesitated, torn between the options of steering the conversation onto neutral ground and just dealing with the issue straight out.

Never one to avoid a problem, he tackled it head-on.

'Apologies aren't my speciality,' he gritted, 'but I think I owe you one. I was unsympathetic and my comments were far too personal—'

'You don't owe me an apology.' She sounded stiff. Formal. And she still didn't look at him. 'You don't have to apologise for being honest. I'm the one who was deluding myself.' The only indication that she was still crying was the way she discreetly lifted her hand to wipe her face, but somehow that minimal gesture increased his feelings of guilt.

'You obviously thought you were acting in the best interests of your sister—' He broke off as he saw her flinch and lift a slender hand to silence him.

'Alessio, please don't say any more. There's only so much honesty I can take in one go.'

He'd been trying to help. But softening the truth wasn't his forte.

Alessio raked his fingers through his hair, stunned by the realisation that for once he was *totally* unsure what he should say next. He was a lawyer. He *always* knew what to say next. 'What I'm trying to say is that you probably—definitely,' he corrected himself swiftly, 'you *definitely* know better than I do what works for Ruby.'

'Apparently not.'

'You're a *great* sister.' Alessio delivered that statement with what he hoped was an appropriate degree of conviction. 'Ruby is lucky to have someone like you watching over her.'

For a moment she didn't answer. Then she wiped her face with her fingers once more, and turned to face him. 'No. Everything you've said is true. I *have* been too controlling. I thought I was protecting her, but I've handled her in the worst way possible. I've done all the wrong things at all the wrong times.'

His hands tightened on her arms. 'For all the right reasons.'

'I've let her down. She's my responsibility, but I've made it impossible for her to turn to me because she knows I'll be upset and worried, and—I've missed the fact that she's grown up...' Her voice wobbled and for a moment she stopped speaking and just breathed.

Waiting for her to finish her sentence, Alessio discovered that her determination not to lose control in front of him was a thousand times more moving than a cascade of tears.

'Lindsay—'

'Don't say anything,' she muttered. 'This is—a bit difficult—' she lifted a hand to her mouth and then let it fall again '—and the reason it's difficult is because everything you say is true. I've failed her.' For some reason the brave smile was a greater attack on his conscience than her tears and Alessio swore softly.

'*Why* do you feel she's your responsibility?'

Lindsay looked at him for a moment. 'Because she's my

little sister,' she whispered, 'and it doesn't matter what she does, she'll always be my little sister.'

'Precisely.' Feeling as though he were drowning, Alessio ran a hand over the back of his neck. 'You're her sister, not her mother.'

'I've always looked after her.' She gave a twisted smile. 'Or, at least, that's what I was trying to do. But it seems I haven't been helping her as much as I thought.'

Alessio inhaled sharply. 'Take no notice of anything I say. As you rightly point out, I know nothing about relationships. Relationships are always complicated, Lindsay—' his tone was harsher than he'd intended '—that's why I avoid them.'

'Do you mind if we don't talk about this anymore right now?' Clearly hanging on to control by a thread, she turned away from him and walked over to the huge blanket. 'It's very dark.'

'It's the storm. It will pass, but probably not before nightfall. We'll be spending the night here.'

He waited for her to have hysterics or make some sharp remark about him having engineered the situation, but she did neither. Instead she simply dropped to her knees onto the blanket and curled up with her back to him.

'If you don't mind, I think I might sleep. I haven't had much sleep since Ruby went missing…' Her voice tailed off and for a moment she hesitated. 'But of course she isn't actually missing, is she? She just doesn't want me to know where she is.'

Lying there, trying to make herself as small as possible, she reminded him of a lost child.

'You must be very angry with her.'

'Angry?' Her voice was thickened with tears. 'How could I possibly be angry with her when it's all my fault? You're quite right. I've driven her away. My behaviour has driven her away.'

Nowhere near as forgiving, Alessio found his own anger

towards Ruby flaring to life. She should have known how much her sister would worry. *She should have picked up the bloody phone.*

It was obvious that Lindsay, however misguided, had genuinely been acting for her sister's benefit and, sensing the depth of her hurt, Alessio gritted his teeth, taking her pain as yet another example of why love was the utter pits. Why did anyone bother? *Who wanted to put themselves through that?* Much better to build a barrier around one's emotions.

And that was what he'd done, of course.

From a very early age.

He sat down next to her. His eyes rested on the smooth skin of her bare shoulder and then followed the line of her red swimsuit. It dipped temptingly into her tiny waist and then rose again to accommodate the feminine swell of her hips. Instinctively he lifted a hand to trace that all too tempting curve, but there was something in the way she held herself that stopped him. Instead, he rolled onto his back and stared up at the ceiling, practising restraint for the first time in his life.

Reminding himself not to express his opinion of her sister ever again, he closed his eyes.

It was going to be a long night.

Lindsay lay in the depths of misery, drowning in self-blame.

This was *all* her fault. She could see that now.

If she'd been more approachable and less judgmental, Ruby would have felt able to confide in her—she would have *called*.

How could she have been so horribly wrong? She spent her working life helping couples see that there were always two points of view, and yet had she ever listened to what Ruby wanted? No, she hadn't. She'd been so afraid that Ruby would choose the wrong path in life that every time her sister had opened her mouth, she'd lectured and dictated. Don't do this—don't do that.

And who was to say that Ruby's choices would have been the wrong ones?

Alessio was right. The wrong path for one person was the right path for another.

Ridden with guilt, Lindsay squeezed her eyes tightly shut. She loved her sister so much. So much. And had she helped her? No.

She was a stupid idiot.

The thought of how badly she'd handled everything was like a physical pain.

She'd been so convinced that her approach was the right one. After what she'd seen as a child, she'd been determined not to follow the same route. And determined not to let her sister follow the same route. But she'd attached such a strong belief to her own strict code that it had prevented her from understanding how others felt. Since when had she become so pompous and set in her ways that she'd decided there was only one right way to do things?

Perhaps Ruby was, at this moment, having the time of her life with Dino Capelli.

Perhaps she wanted to share that happiness and excitement, and the reason she wasn't calling Ruby was because she knew she wouldn't approve.

Would Ruby ever turn to her again?

Tears slid down her face and this time she didn't bother trying to stop them because it was dark and Alessio was asleep.

Convinced that she was alone with her misery, she gave a start of shock as a strong male hand curved over her shoulder.

'*Stop* crying.'

Appalled that he knew she was crying, Lindsay froze. 'I'm not crying.'

He muttered something in Italian. 'I tell you now,' he said roughly, 'I have absolutely *no* experience in comforting women. It isn't something I excel at. Ask anyone.' He hesitated. 'Normally I'm the one making them cry.'

Lindsey gave a choked laugh. 'I can believe that. But for once you're not to blame. Everything you said is right. I might even get round to thanking you at some point. And you don't need to worry—I don't want comfort.' She sniffed and scrubbed a hand over her face, relieved that it was dark. 'Anyway, I thought you had to be the best at everything.'

'Only the things that interest me. Strangely enough I have no ambitions to excel at drying women's tears,' he drawled softly, 'but on this one occasion, given that I'm the cause of your upset, I'm prepared to make an exception.'

Realising just how great a sacrifice that was on his part, she almost managed to smile. This must be almost as bad for him as it was for her. 'You're not the cause. Go to sleep, Alessio.'

But his strong, warm hand didn't move from her shoulder. 'This rug is the only dry thing in the place and I'd like to keep it that way. *Stop* feeling guilty about your sister.'

'Why?' She mumbled the words, wondering why she was discussing it with him. Alessio Capelli wasn't anyone's idea of a perfect confidant. 'It's *all* my fault.'

'It isn't your fault. I keep telling you, Ruby is responsible for what she does.'

'I've stopped her talking to me.'

'And what if she *had* talked to you? You would have been given a running commentary on all her wild behaviour and it would have driven you crazy with stress. You wouldn't have said anything, but you still would have felt it. You're much better off not knowing.' His tone rang with exasperation and she almost laughed.

'You make it sound so easy.'

'It *is* easy. It's time to toughen up, Lindsay,' he said gruffly. 'How have you managed to get through the past two decades when you worry so much about everything?'

'I don't really worry—'

'You're avoiding life because you're afraid of it.'

Lindsay stilled. 'That isn't true.'

'You're worried that your sister will be hurt and maybe she will—' his voice was low and male in the darkness '—but maybe she will have an affair that she will remember for ever. Memories of real passion that will last long after the hurt has faded. What will you have, Lindsay? The memory of dangerously exciting moments that you successfully resisted?'

He was right, she realised painfully. She *was* afraid. Afraid of falling into the same trap as the couples she counselled, afraid of being drawn into the wrong decision, *afraid of being like her mother*....

She wiped her tears with the back of her hand. 'You live dangerously all the time. So how do you manage never to be hurt?'

'I don't let people get close.'

'But what sort of life is that?'

There was a moment of silence and then he gave a hollow laugh. 'I'm not the one lying on the rug crying, Lindsay.'

'Caring for people and having people care about you is the only really important thing in life.' It was just because it was dark, she told herself, that it was easy to talk to him.

'And is it worth caring even when you get hurt?'

'Even then. It's what makes us human.'

'Ah—but you told me only a few days ago that I'm not human, so that explains why we think differently.'

She could hear the trace of humour in his voice. 'I thought life was straightforward. But everything suddenly seems so complicated.'

'Relationships always are. That's why I avoid them.'

'But you can't just go through life avoiding relationships. Relationships—love—well, that's what makes life bearable, isn't it?'

'Relationships—maybe. Love? Definitely not. In fact I'd go as far as to say that love is probably one of the things that often makes life *un*bearable. Believe me, I see it all the time.'

'But the people you see aren't in love anymore. Perhaps they never were.'

'There are other types of relationships.'

'I know. And that's where I've let Ruby down,' Lindsay admitted, relieved that it was dark so that he couldn't see her face. Somehow the dark made it easier to talk. 'We're very different like that. I was always worried that she would confuse chemistry with love and I've seen so many relationships fall apart because all the couple shared was chemistry. I've never contemplated being in a relationship that was just about sex.'

It was a moment before he answered and when he finally spoke his voice was soft in the darkness.

'Haven't you?'

A shiver of awareness ripped through her whole body and she didn't pretend to misunderstand him.

'Well—maybe I have. Once.' Her heart was thumping and bumping against her chest, as if it were trying to escape while there was still a chance.

His fingers tightened on her shoulder. 'You have willpower that most people would envy.'

'If you're talking about us, then we would have been a nightmare together, you know we would.'

He gave a low laugh and rolled her gently onto her back. 'It would have been explosive, *tesoro*. And you know it. Which is why you've been holding back. What's wrong with sexual attraction, Lindsay?'

'Nothing, as long as both parties recognise it for what it is. Ruby doesn't.'

This was the time that she should push him away. This was the time she should tell him that, although she'd realised she'd handled Ruby all wrong, she didn't want to change the way she lived herself. She wasn't about to hurl herself from a place of safety into the dangerous unknown of raw sexual excitement.

She should tell him that. She should tell him that *right now*.

But she couldn't manage to form the words. Instead her hand slid over his shoulder, feeling the hard curve of male muscle under her seeking fingers.

This level of chemistry wasn't something she'd ever experienced before—and probably never would again.

If she let it pass, would she regret it?

Would she look back in her old age and think, *If only?*

Or would she smile and tell her grandchildren that passion wasn't always dangerous, as long as you recognised it for what it was?

There would be no 'happy ever after' with Alessio Capelli, but she knew that, didn't she? It wasn't a mistake. It was a choice.

'Lindsay—' The husky, questioning note in his voice made her realise that her hand had curved around his neck.

She sensed that he was holding back—*that this was all up to her*—but she had no more time to agonise over her decision because her hands were drawing his head towards hers.

Apparently it was all the encouragement he needed because he instantly took control, his hands not quite steady as he rolled her onto her back and covered her body with his.

It seemed that her senses still remembered how he'd kissed her on the beach, and a pool of heat coiled itself in her pelvis and she waited in an agony of anticipation for the slow, skilled assault of his mouth.

Only this time he didn't give her slow.

This time he brought his mouth down on hers with a driven sense of purpose that propelled her from a state of simmering anticipation to explosive excitement. Hot with longing, she felt him cup her face with lean, strong hands and then part her lips with his tongue. He took her mouth with devastating expertise, his demanding and intimate exploration creating erotic curls of heat low in her pelvis.

It was like being drugged and her last coherent thought

was, *How did he learn to kiss like this?* Before she slid down and down into a sensual world that was beyond her control.

Her senses connected like an electric circuit, sending sparks to every part of her and she was lost, totally lost.

She pressed herself against his hard, powerful body, felt the roughness of his thigh graze against the softness of hers, felt the scrape of stubble against her cheek as he dragged his mouth from hers only to bury it in her neck.

'Alessio—I can't wait—don't wait—' She writhed, lost in the sensation he was creating. 'Please—' But her plea turned to a moan as she felt his mouth fasten over the pink, throbbing tip of her breast. Up until that moment she hadn't even realised that he'd removed her costume and suddenly she was aware that she was naked. But the feeling that engulfed her wasn't embarrassment, but desperation.

It seemed that the more he touched her, the more she wanted, and when she felt his hand reach down between her thighs she gave a low moan of encouragement that changed to a gasp as she felt the skilled slide of his fingers.

She felt wild, desperate and totally unlike herself, writhing against him as she tried to relieve the unbearable ache in her pelvis.

'You feel *so* good, *tesoro*,' Alessio groaned and then gently moved his hand, cupped her bottom and positioned her to his satisfaction.

For a breathless moment she felt the hot, silken tip of his erection against her, and then he brought his mouth down on hers again and entered her with a series of controlled thrusts that drove the breath from her body. He was big, *so big* that for a moment she tensed, and he must have sensed her sudden apprehension because he paused for a moment and lifted his mouth from hers just enough to speak.

'I'm hurting you?'

'No, I—no—'

'Then relax, *tesoro*,' he instructed huskily, 'and let your body do what it is desperate to do.' But he lowered his mouth to hers again and kissed her until the explicit movement of his tongue in her mouth made her rake her fingers over the smooth muscle of his shoulders.

She whimpered deep in her throat and he lifted her hips and sank himself deep inside her, his eyes half-open as he watched her abandoned response. And then he withdrew slightly and did it again, creating waves of pure pulsing pleasure that consumed her entire body.

Completely out of control, she clung to him, her cries smothered by his mouth, her body hovering on the edge of ecstasy as he drove her higher and higher. And then finally, when she thought she couldn't possibly go on any longer, her body exploded around him and the rhythmic pulse of her moist flesh drove him to his own completion.

Alessio held her firmly as he surged into her over and over again and his rhythmic thrusts prolonged her own sensual ecstasy until the whole experience became one long shower of intolerable excitement.

He woke to sunshine and silence and even before he turned his head to glance around the room, he knew he was alone.

The storm had blown itself out and bright shards of sunlight shone like spotlights through the windows of the cottage.

But there was no Lindsay.

Experienced in the art of shifting reluctant women from his bed, Alessio found it something of a surprise to realise that at some point Lindsay had actually left without disturbing him.

The fact that she hadn't waited around for soft words or even a repeat performance, astonished him. He waited to feel relieved but instead he felt a thud of—

What, exactly?

Disappointment?

Well, of course, disappointment. Just as he'd predicted, it had been the most explosive sexual encounter of his life and he'd had no intention of restricting himself to one night.

Slightly irritated that they couldn't have started the day the way they'd ended it, Alessio sprang to his feet, retrieved his swimming shorts and glanced around the cottage.

Exactly when had she left? And why?

It wasn't as if she hadn't enjoyed the experience. Remembering her soft cries and passionate response, he gave a slow smile. She'd definitely enjoyed the experience—which made her absence all the more strange.

Yanking open the door, he strode out onto the beach that had been the venue for her trauma the night before. A few pieces of driftwood had been washed up in the storm but the sea was now idyllically calm. And there was no sign of Lindsay.

A faint frown touching his brows, Alessio strode across the soft sand and followed the curve of the bay back towards the cove where he'd secured the boat. The sky was a perfect blue, the sun dazzling, it was as if the storm of the night before had never happened.

A splash drew his attention and Alessio saw a flash of blonde hair and creamy female skin. It was Lindsay, and she was swimming far out in the bay. As he watched she dived under the surface again and vanished.

In the grip of a serious attack of lust, Alessio strode purposefully into the waves, plunged under the water and powered his way over to where she was snorkelling.

'Oh—' She surfaced with a gasp, her hair sleek and wet against her head, a bright smile on her face. 'You made me jump! It's such a beautiful day.'

That was it? *That was all she was going to say?*

'*Buon giorno.*' He watched with masculine satisfaction as the colour bloomed in her cheeks, but still she made no reference to what had happened the previous night.

Instead she dragged her gaze from his and concentrated on staring down into the water. 'It's *so* clear—I've never seen anything like this. I just couldn't resist having another go before we leave. Snorkelling is just the *best* thing.'

Not quite the best thing, Alessio thought to himself idly, his attention suddenly captured by the droplets of water on her soft mouth. Her lower lip was a full, generous curve. Remembering just how good she tasted, he was about to kiss her when she dived under the water again.

Simmering with frustration and tormented by the nagging throb of his body, Alessio cursed softly and wondered why it was that Lindsay continually surprised him.

During his walk from the cottage to the beach, he'd prepared himself to handle various different emotions from her—embarrassment, affection, *regret*?

The one thing that he hadn't expected was that she'd make no reference to what they'd shared. At the very least, he'd resigned himself to a conversation about what had happened between them.

There were women, of course, who could enjoy the passionate encounter they'd experienced the night before and move on without a word.

But Lindsay wasn't that sort of woman.

Frowning slightly, he watched as she surfaced again.

'I saw a shoal of clownfish next to the reef! Honestly, Alessio, this is just the best thing I've ever done.' Wiping the water from her face, she smiled at him. 'Aren't you going to swim?'

Swim?

Simmering with suppressed sexual tension, Alessio searched her wide blue eyes for signs that she was creating this torture on purpose. But there was no flirtatious twinkle or wicked gleam, and in the end he was forced to admit that she *obviously* had absolutely no idea of the effect she was having on him.

Which gave him a whole new problem. Usually at this point in a relationship, the woman in question was snuggled against him, already planning a future that wasn't going to happen. *Usually* his problem was extracting himself, so it came as something of a shock to discover that he had no desire whatsoever to extricate himself from Lindsay.

Distinctly unsettled by just how badly he wanted to drag her back to the cottage, Alessio dipped down under the surface of the water, consoling himself with the fact that it was perfectly natural to want her again. While it was true that he didn't exactly embrace long relationships, neither did he indulge in one-night stands. So everything he was feeling was entirely normal.

He just needed to get her back in his bed until—well, until he no longer wanted her in his bed.

Simple.

CHAPTER EIGHT

EXHAUSTED from the lack of sleep, a night of rampant sex and the stress of acting a part, Lindsay sat in the bow of the yacht, facing forwards. The energy required to behave in a bright, happy mood had completely sapped the last of her reserves.

She barely even remembered the storm. For her, the hurricane had been inside her, a wind of change, blowing aside her all her old beliefs and leaving them wrecked and in pieces.

She felt—*she felt*—

Lindsay lifted her chin and turned her face to the sun. She wasn't going to ask herself how she felt. She didn't *dare* ask herself how she felt because she didn't want to know the answer.

And what difference did it make, anyway?

He wasn't going to be interested in her feelings. Alessio Capelli didn't do feelings. She knew that. He was famous for it, wasn't he? No ties. No emotions.

And she wasn't going to allow herself to mind that he hadn't once mentioned what had happened the previous night—*hadn't even kissed her.*

For a brief, disturbing moment her mind flickered back to the intensity of what they'd shared and she clutched the rail more tightly.

'Lindsay, come here.' His cool command sent shivers of awareness down her spine and for a moment she hesitated.

She wasn't actually sure that she had the energy to keep up the pretence of normality. But if she didn't go—

Forcing herself to think neutral thoughts, she turned and strolled to the back of the boat.

He handled the boat with confidence and a sure touch, dark glasses shading his eyes from the harsh rays of the sun. 'You need to wear a hat. You'll burn.' Reaching down, he picked up a hat and slipped it onto her head in a decisive gesture. 'You're very fair. You need to be careful.'

Careful?

Lindsay swallowed back the hysterical laugh that almost burst from her throat. *Careful?* If she'd wanted to be careful, then she wouldn't have spent the night the way she had. What they'd shared hadn't been remotely careful. It had been reckless, wild and totally abandoned. 'I thought you were encouraging me to take more risks.'

'Sunburn is a certainty,' he drawled, 'not a risk. And it's painful.'

Suddenly she was grateful for the hat. She pulled at the wide brim, shading her features and, hopefully, her facial expression. And she wondered what had made her naïvely think that she'd be able to share one incredible night with him and then walk away as if nothing had happened.

Unable to stop herself, Lindsay risked a sideways glance at him and immediately her eyes collided with his penetrating dark gaze. Her insides tumbled, flames licked through her body and she turned away quickly, knowing that she'd embarrass herself if she looked at him any longer.

No clinging, no sighing and no long, desperate looks, she reminded herself desperately. She'd known it was just for one night.

But when they'd finally connected in the most intimate way possible, she'd wanted it to be for always.

And she knew it was because she was in love with him.

She'd known it the moment she awoke and found herself in his arms. For her, it had always been so much more than chemistry. Perhaps she'd always been a little bit in love with him, ever since that evening when he'd come to her rescue.

So in the end, she'd been true to herself, hadn't she?

Her choice had been sex with love, even though that love wasn't returned.

Love.

Horrified that he'd see something in her expression, Lindsay kept her eyes fixed on the horizon, desperately hoping that his expertise with women didn't run to reading minds.

'Are we going to talk about this?' His voice was a deep, dark drawl and she kept her eyes on the water, trying to forget the way he'd sounded when he'd breathed soft words of encouragement to her during the night.

'Talk about what?'

'Oh, well, let's see—perhaps because you spent the night having wild sex with a wicked divorce lawyer who you don't approve of. That might give most women pause for thought.'

'I made my choice.'

'You made your choice when you were in an extremely emotional state. Those circumstances frequently lead to regret.'

'I don't regret anything.' And it was true. She would have done the same thing again. Yes, she'd been upset. Confused. Emotional. But for that one night she'd also been—curious. She'd wanted to give in to the amazing chemistry between them and see where it led.

She'd wanted to have that one moment. And now, for the first time, she understood what made other people act in a reckless fashion.

She *really* understood.

Was this how her mother had felt?

Lindsay stood still, thinking about her mother as a woman for the first time. A sexual woman.

'Lindsay?'

She dragged her mind back from the confusing mists of her childhood and realised that Alessio was watching her intently. And she knew that even if nothing but pain was to follow, she would have done exactly the same thing again if she'd been given the choice. 'I'm not blaming you, if that's what you're worried about.'

Suddenly she was relieved that she'd made the decision to get up before he awoke. It had removed the temptation to snuggle against him and initiate the type of intimacy that she knew he hated.

It had also removed the utter embarrassment of having to face him for the first time in the revealing spotlight of the morning sunshine.

'Lindsay—'

'Can we talk about something else?' She interrupted him quickly, adjusting the hat again simply because she needed to do something with her hands. *Something other than sliding them round his neck.* 'I completely understand that being trapped on a boat with the woman you spent the night before with must be your idea of a nightmare. But you *really* needn't worry. I don't want to talk about it either.'

She waited for him to give some indication that he was grateful for her sensitivity, but he simply studied her in brooding silence until the longing inside her became so acute that she knew that if she didn't move away she'd do something that would embarrass both of them.

Alessio Capelli has taught me everything about passion, she thought desperately, *but what he hasn't taught me is how to walk away afterwards.*

Three hours later Lindsay lay in a luxuriously scented bath, staring at an unbroken view of smooth white sand and palm trees.

She felt drained after the emotional battering she'd

received over the past twenty-four hours, but, strangely enough, she also felt calmer than she'd felt in years.

For the first time ever her heart rate stayed steady when she thought about her mother.

And when she thought of Ruby it was with resignation rather than desperation.

And as for herself—

On the bed next door was her dress, laid out ready for the evening. It was the simplest dress in her new wardrobe. Powder-blue and summery rather than sexy. And that suited her.

The last thing she wanted was Alessio thinking she was trying to engender a repeat performance.

She was painfully aware that if they hadn't been trapped on an island, she wouldn't be seeing him again. And clearly he was finding their continued proximity a major cause of irritation.

They'd arrived back at Kingfisher Cay just before lunch. Alessio had immediately leaped from the boat onto the narrow wooden jetty, paused to exchange a few words with the staff member hovering ready to take the boat, and then strode off to his villa without so much as a single smouldering glance in her direction.

It was obvious from his body language that he had no desire to spend another moment in her company.

And had that hurt?

Yes. It had been agony, because no matter how many times she told herself that this was what she'd expected, she'd still *wanted* something entirely different.

Lindsay sniffed and slowly rubbed the bubbles over her skin. Even though she knew exactly who he was and the rules he played by, she was still human enough—*female enough*—to have wished that he'd swept her into his arms, carried her to the nearest private place and demanded a repeat performance.

But Alessio Capelli didn't do repeat performances, did he?

She slid farther under the bubbles, trying to ignore the recurrent buzz of electricity coursing through her body. It was as if he'd flicked a switch, but hadn't bothered to turn it off again afterwards.

And now she had to live with the consequences.

The next time she chose to have a wild fling, she was going to make sure that she'd planned her escape route. Instead of both being able to go their own ways, pretending that nothing had happened, they were both trapped here in paradise— forced to confront each other. And everything about the setting was designed to make that as hard as possible.

Kingfisher Cay was designed for romance. From its curved soft beaches, to the privacy of its coves, it was a place for lovers.

Exasperated with herself, Lindsay stepped out of the bath and reached for one of the large, soft towels that had been laid out ready for her use.

Stupid, stupid, stupid.

She'd *known* what he was like.

She wasn't going to turn into one of those sad, deluded women who thought they'd be the one to make a bad boy change his wicked ways.

Wrapping the towel around her body, she sat on the edge of the bath, staring blindly at the smooth, tiled floor.

So that, she thought numbly, was that.

One night with Alessio Capelli.

And now she had to play the game until she could escape from Kingfisher Cay and back to her old life.

A tap on the door made her heart rate double, but it was just Natalya, smiling an apology for having disturbed her.

'Signor Capelli requests your presence for drinks at the Beach Club at seven.'

Lindsay's heart performed a series of leaps, but she some-how managed to nod. Horrified by the sudden flash of excite-ment that came from the realisation that she was going to spend an evening in his company, Lindsay watched Natalya go and gave herself a sharp talking-to.

But despite her best efforts to rein it in, her mind was racing ahead.

He couldn't be that anxious to remove her from his presence, could he? Not if he was inviting her to join him at the Beach Club for the evening?

The Beach Club at night was the most romantic setting. Built on stilts, the glass floor extended over the shallow water of the cove, allowing guests to feel as though they were walking on the clear, illuminated water. During the day, guests swam up to the bar for a drink; at night it was transformed by flickering candles, soft music, food designed to take the palate on a roller-coaster ride of gastronomic bliss. It was a lovers' paradise.

And he wanted her to join him there.

She was going to have another night with him.

All right, so another night wasn't a lifetime, but it was something and it was *now*.

Lindsay dried her hair and walked past the powder-blue dress on the bed. Heart thumping, she reached into the wardrobe and pulled out the sexy red silk dress that she'd fingered in awe on the first day.

The old Lindsay would never have worn that dress. But she wasn't the old Lindsay anymore, was she?

She felt—different.

She felt like seizing the moment. Even if it was only one more night, she wanted to make the most of it.

Her hands shaking, she slid it over her scented skin, smoothed it over her hips and then looked at herself in the mirror.

Yes. Oh, yes.

The dress was *desperately* sexy. Feminine, confident— totally unlike anything she'd ever worn before.

And that was fine. Because she didn't feel the way she'd ever felt before.

She was going to spend an evening at the Kingfisher Cay Beach Club with Alessio Capelli. It was right that she should look glamorous.

Lindsay applied her make-up, slid her feet into a pair of amazing red silk shoes and took a last look in the mirror.

She barely recognised herself.

On impulse she leaned forward and removed one of the scarlet flowers from the vase on the table. Snapping off the stem, she slid it into her hair and secured it with a pin.

Feeling confident, sexy and excited, she picked up her bag and walked along the path that wound its way towards the Beach Club, smiling as she anticipated Alessio's reaction to her transformation.

Her excitement lasted right up until the moment she saw him.

He was leaning on the bar looking every inch the billionaire tycoon. Broad-shouldered and powerful, he was deep in conversation with a tall, handsome man who looked extremely familiar.

Lindsay's heart lurched.

Oh, no—

She knew instinctively that this man must be Alessio's mysterious and elusive client and the reason he looked familiar was because he was a major Hollywood film star whose films she'd seen on many occasions.

And it was immediately obvious to her that Alessio hadn't invited her for a romantic evening at all.

He'd invited her because his client had arrived.

Lindsay stopped dead, wanting to slink back to her villa, but knowing that if she moved they'd see her.

What was she supposed to do?

It felt surreal, seeing such a famous man in person, when she was used to seeing him on the big screen. Remembering that guaranteed privacy was one of the many benefits of Kingfisher Cay, Lindsay felt a flash of panic and wondered whether she'd better leave.

The rich and famous obviously had a silent pact not to betray the whereabouts of their set, but she wasn't one of them, was she?

Uncertain and uncomfortable, she was just about to retreat when Alessio lifted his dark head and saw her.

For a moment his eyes locked on hers, then they slid slowly down over her bare shoulders and down over the dips and curves of her body accentuated so lovingly by the bold red dress.

Heart thumping, Lindsay waited in breathless anticipation for his reaction, but when he finally lifted his eyes back to hers they were blank of expression.

Nothing.

Instead he lifted a hand and beckoned her over and she went, of course, because the delicious red dress was already drawing attention that she didn't want, and because he wasn't the sort of man you said 'no' to.

It was ironic, she thought miserably, that the only man she'd wanted to notice her didn't appear to be noticing her.

She'd got it so, so wrong.

He hadn't invited her to spend a romantic evening with him. He was expecting her to join in a meeting with his client. But what was still *more* embarrassing was the undeniable fact that he was aware of her mistake. That one single glance had told him that she was dressed for sex and passion, which accounted for the tightening of his hard mouth and the sudden cooling of his gaze.

Alessio knew.

In her mind she could hear him saying, 'You should be so lucky, *tesoro*. You had your one night. That was it.'

Mortified, Lindsay was too busy wishing she could crawl back to her villa and hide to feel remotely star struck by meeting the famous actor.

Telling herself that the presence of another person would make the whole difficult evening a great deal easier, Lindsay joined them, noticing that if anything this huge star was even more handsome in real life than he was on the screen. His eyes were bluer and shone with a hint of humour that was usually absent in the roles he played.

Lindsay glanced around her, expecting the other guests to be staring, but then she realised that the people who came here were all similarly famous. She recognised the lead singer from an extremely famous rock band, a supermodel and a billionaire industrialist who was never out of the news.

In this company, the 'A' list actor blended comfortably.

She was the odd one out.

It felt surreal, sipping her drink next to a man whose love life had been played out across the pages of the world's gossip magazines.

Desperately miserable, Lindsay glanced briefly at Alessio, and then wished she hadn't because once her eyes rested on the sharp lines of his profile it was impossible to look away.

The actor was outlining his personal situation and Alessio angled his dark head, his gaze sharp and acute as he sifted through the facts. *You can almost see his brain working*, Lindsay thought helplessly, watching his unwavering focus on his client. His astonishing intelligence was evident, not only in the observations that he made, but also in the sharp glitter of his eyes and in every line of his hard, handsome features. He was clever. Clever and strong.

Lindsay's eyes drifted to the dark shadow of his jaw. He was a man to whom decision-making came easily. Not for him the agonies of 'shall I shan't I' suffered by lesser mortals. No wonder people trusted him with their darkest secrets and their biggest problems. He was coldly analytical and decisive, which explained why he wasn't remotely impressed or intimidated by the presence of Hollywood's favourite film star.

Most men would have faded into the background.

Not Alessio.

Lindsay smiled politely as Alessio introduced them,

fighting down a spurt of panic as she realised that, although she was with one of America's biggest film stars, the only man she wanted to stare at was Alessio.

The Sicilian lawyer was actually more startlingly handsome than the man whose presence on the screen had made him the object of fantasy for millions of women worldwide.

Deciding that the only way she was going to make it through the evening was to not look at him, or think about him, Lindsay focused all her attention on the actor and his situation.

So *he* was the one contemplating divorce—

Does his wife know? she wondered. Or was this just an exploratory meeting to ascertain how much a divorce was going to cost him?

'I should have listened to the old saying—marry in haste, repent at leisure.' He drained his glass of champagne. 'Good sex is never a reason to get married.'

'You sound uncannily like Lindsay,' Alessio said in a cool tone, a sardonic gleam in his eyes as he glanced at her. 'She doesn't approve of relationships based on sex.'

'On the contrary—' she lifted her head and smiled '—I have no problem with relationships based on sex, providing the parties involved understand that physical chemistry alone isn't a good basis for marriage. If sex is all you have in common, then fine. Just don't get married.'

'That's the best advice anyone has ever given me. I only wish I'd met you a couple of years ago. You would have saved me a fortune.' Draining his glass, the actor looked at her thoughtfully. 'I take it you're not married?'

'No.'

'And you have no problem with relationships based on sex.'

Was it her imagination or was this gorgeous man who was famed for his liaisons with equally gorgeous women actually smiling at her? *Flirting with her?*

'I think it's important to be realistic.'

'Where have you been all my life?' The actor was laughing now, a look of sexy invitation in those famous blue eyes. 'How long are you here for? Come and spend some time with me in Los Angeles after you leave. I'll show you the sights.'

'I might just do that.' Desperately miserable about Alessio and feeling suddenly reckless, Lindsay smiled back at him. Reckless? Since when had reckless been an adjective that applied to her? A week ago she'd never done anything reckless in her life. Now she seemed to be doing nothing but reckless things.

And on top of that it suddenly seemed desperately important to show Alessio that she wasn't pining. He'd barely glanced in her direction and the message he was sending her had come across loud and clear.

Not interested.

Unlike the actor who barely seemed able to drag his eyes away from her face and body, Alessio seemed hardly to notice her presence. He didn't address her directly, his gaze didn't once linger on her bare shoulder or her cleavage and he seemed totally relaxed.

Clearly whatever wild chemistry had possessed him before last night had been extinguished by the heat of that one single encounter.

For him, there was nothing left.

Suddenly it seemed incredibly important for her pride and self-esteem that he didn't realise just how bad she felt.

And to be fair, it wasn't exactly his fault that she felt bad, was it?

He hadn't once lied to her. He hadn't promised her anything.

He'd been completely true to his nature, which was to keep relationships light and easy.

She was the one who'd broken the rules—by expecting something she couldn't have.

The actor was gazing at her mouth with ill-concealed fascination. 'Have you ever been to Hollywood?'

'Perhaps we ought to dispense with your current wife before you contemplate a replacement,' Alessio drawled in a soft tone, putting his empty glass on the bar and gesturing towards a table that had been reserved for them in the most secluded area of the Beach Club. 'Shall we eat?'

Sensing his black mood, Lindsay glanced at him nervously. Was he still annoyed that she'd misinterpreted the whole situation and dressed for a romantic evening?

His client didn't seem bothered.

In fact he continued to flirt outrageously.

As the staff served them discreetly Alessio turned the conversation to the issue of divorce and asked a number of blunt, specific questions about the actor's marriage. Very much the lawyer, he was brief and businesslike, reducing the relationship to a series of cold facts.

Lindsay concentrated on her food, listening while Alessio dealt with the actor's questions and then summarised his options.

She didn't feel the slightest inclination to intervene or even urge him to reconsider. What did she know about relationships? After last night, she'd decided that she knew nothing.

And that, Lindsay thought bleakly, *was that.*

Another celebrity marriage bit the dust.

The actor sat back in his chair, his eyes on the gentle curve and dip of Lindsay's cleavage. 'Well, if we're done, Alessio, I feel like relaxing. You've no idea how amazing it feels to be able to chill out, knowing that for once your evening is not going to be replayed in the morning papers. Can you spare your assistant for the rest of the evening?'

'I'm afraid not. She has work to do.' Alessio's tone was smooth and his eyes blank of expression, but something in his manner delivered his message loud and clear because the actor gave a frown and then shrugged.

'OK. Some other time.' His eyes lingered on Lindsay's mouth. 'Don't leave without taking my number.'

'Your number is in the file.' Very much the one in control, Alessio rose to his feet and extended a hand. 'My team will contact you when you're back in L.A. Enjoy your stay. And try not to marry your next co-star.'

Feeling increasingly awkward, Lindsay stood up as well and stammered a goodnight.

And finally, Alessio looked at her. 'My villa.' It was a cool command. 'I want to work on this straight away.'

And it was obvious that he was annoyed with her, Lindsay thought miserably as she followed him up a path that led to a villa out of sight of the rest of the exclusive resort.

He was going to remind her that it had been just the one night.

He didn't want to see glamorous red dresses or flowers in her hair.

Too tense even to react to the luxurious villa or the stunning setting, she flinched as he yanked open the sliding doors that led from beach to living room.

'Nice,' she muttered timidly and then felt suddenly angry with herself because she'd never allowed herself to be intimidated by him before and she just *hated* the fact that she felt like that now. By nature honest, she decided that it was best to come clean, however awkward that might be. 'Look—it was a misunderstanding, all right? When I received your message I thought—' She broke off and he lifted a brow.

'You thought what? That this was your chance to join the ranks of Hollywood?'

Taken aback by this unexpected verbal attack, Lindsay just stared at him. 'What are you talking about?'

Dark colour accentuated his cheekbones and he prowled across to her, his eyes stormy. 'I'm talking about you flirting with my client. I'm talking about the flower in your hair, the sexy red dress and the killer heels. *That's* what I'm talking about, Lindsay.'

Her gaze locked with his, she suddenly couldn't breathe.

He thought the dress was sexy?

Even though she could feel the atmosphere sparking dangerously, she felt a wild thrill of pleasure.

'Alessio—'

His hands were on her shoulders, tight bands of steel. 'I'm talking about the fact that you're a relationship counsellor, but you didn't once try and talk him out of his divorce. Not once.' His handsome face hard and unyielding, he powered her back against the enormous bed that dominated the room until she tumbled backwards onto the silken cover.

'Alessio—'

He came down on top of her, bronzed, muscular and very much the dominant male. '*Why* didn't you try and talk him out of divorce?' One strong hand buried itself in her hair and he kept his gaze locked with hers. 'Why was that, *tesoro*? Was it because you were hoping that you might be the next candidate?'

'Don't be ridiculous—' Lindsay stared up at him with huge, shocked eyes. Her heart thudding out of control, explosions of excitement turning her body into a simmering cauldron of dangerous sensation. '*You* were the one who told me that you didn't want me here in my role as relationship counsellor—'

'You dressed for sex. What happened to those principles of yours?' With a decisive movement, he slid a hand under her bottom and hauled her against the thickened ridge of his arousal. 'What happened, *tesoro*? You meet a film star and suddenly a relationship based on sex seems like a good idea?'

All she could feel was heat. The heat of his body. The heat of his mouth next to hers. *The heat of her own desperate need—*

'Alessio—' Her words were smothered by the force of his kiss, his mouth taking hers in a punishing, demanding, volcanic assault that tipped her into a sensual world that was entirely new to her.

The hot slide of his tongue in her mouth sent a shaft of excitement shooting from brain to belly and her hands clutched at his shirt, tugging it free from his trousers.

She wasn't thinking. She was no longer *able* to think. It was all about instinct. Primal, animal instinct.

Swearing in Italian, Alessio shifted his weight so that he had full access to her body. Then he pushed her dress up to her waist in a rough, impatient movement that drew a gasp of shocked excitement from her parted lips.

With no concession to modesty, he slid a demanding hand over her bared body and then pushed her thighs apart and buried his mouth against the most private part of her.

Lindsay choked out a protest, but he held her with firm, confident hands, his mouth warm against the dampened silk of her panties. Then his fingers curled into the flimsy material and he gave a forceful yank, removing that final barrier with determined fingers before focusing all his attention on that one single part of her that he'd exposed specifically for his pleasure.

She felt as though she were back in the storm, the entire force of nature directing its power onto her.

His fingers gentled as he parted her and then she felt the warm, moist flick of his tongue caressing her *there* and it felt so wickedly good, *so maddeningly, impossibly exciting*, that for a moment the world went black.

And then her body exploded into a climax so intense that her hands clutched frantically at the sheets and her body arched against his skilful mouth.

Weakened and dizzy, she barely had time to catch her breath before he shifted again, this time so that he was over her, once again in a position of domination. His shirt was hanging loose where she'd torn at it and he reached down and dealt with the zip of his trousers with an impatient hand.

There was a breathless moment of anticipation when she felt the hard silken promise of his masculinity and then he entered her with such a possessive, powerful thrust that her body immediately spun out of control again. Her second climax was as powerful as the first and she heard him groan in disbelief as the rhythmic contractions of her body added to the delicious friction created by his own thrusts. It was blisteringly hot, terrifying and thrilling all at the same time, her body controlled by the primal rhythm he'd set.

And for Lindsay the pleasure didn't just peak, it went on and on in a glorious shower of ecstasy that was heightened by the warm, silken thickness of his arousal deep inside her.

She wanted to cry out, but she was robbed of breath and she felt his arm slide under her hips, lifting her, demanding still more from her quivering, helplessly aroused body. He surged into her again and then again, each thrust increasing the incredible intimacy and she was so overwhelmed by the power and strength of him, so utterly dominated by his aggressive sexuality and devastating masculinity that she had no choice but to go where he led her.

'You're incredible and you feel *so* good—' He growled the words against her mouth, his voice unsteady as he drove himself deeper. Groaning something in Italian, he slid a hand up her thigh, encouraging her to wrap her legs around him. 'Sexy, sexy woman—'

Was she?

Maybe she was. All she knew was that her body didn't feel like her own anymore.

The excitement was so intense that she was almost blind with it, her body meeting the urgent demands of his with the same desperate compulsion that he obviously felt.

It went on and on, explosion after explosion until she was wild with it, until she could do nothing but rake her nails over the smooth muscle of his powerful shoulders, holding on to the one thing that seemed solid. Again and again she lost control and finally he lost control right along with her, thrusting deeply, filling her with the explosive force of his climax.

For endless moments neither of them spoke or moved.

Lindsay lay there stunned, eyes closed, her heart so full of emotion that it stole her breath.

His head was still buried against her shoulder and his breathing was harsh and uneven. Suddenly her fingers ached to stroke that thick, glossy hair. She desperately wanted to lean her face into his shoulder and kiss him, not with passion, but with love.

There were things she wanted to whisper to him.

She wanted to tell him how she felt.

But that wasn't allowed, was it?

That wasn't part of the deal.

So she squeezed her eyes tightly shut and forced herself to swallow back all the words that wanted to spill out of her mouth.

And what was there to say anyway? What could words possibly add to what they'd just shared? Their connection had been total. Their intimacy complete. She'd expressed her feelings through her body. She'd given *everything* and he'd taken and given right back. Everything.

So in the end she hadn't been able to have sex without love.

She hadn't been capable of that.

Alessio lifted his head. She could feel him looking at her, but she didn't dare open her eyes because of what she might reveal.

Then he rolled onto his back and pulled her firmly into his arms, his vastly superior strength giving her no opportunity to resist.

Her head was nestled against his shoulder and her hand lingered on the hard muscle of his abdomen. 'I should go back to my villa—'

'You're not moving.' His grip tightened on her. 'Except perhaps to stand up and remove that dress. From now on when you're in my bed, I want you naked.'

'Alessio—'

'I don't understand you,' he confessed in a raw tone. 'You spend your whole life preaching about how sex should be part of a committed relationship and every time we make love, you try to dash off.'

'We're not in a committed relationship,' she muttered, her heart thumping crazily. 'You don't do relationships.'

'Neither do I do one-night stands.' He turned onto his side and cupped her cheek with his hand, forcing her to look at him. 'And you're not doing them, either.'

She stilled. 'I—I thought that was what you wanted.'

His eyes narrowed. 'That's why you were leaving? Because you thought it was what I wanted?'

'Of course. I didn't want to embarrass you by still being around in the morning.'

He gave a slow, devilish smile. 'Do I look embarrassed?'

'You hate morning-after conversation.'

'Who said anything about conversation?' he drawled softly, rolling her onto her back again and bringing his mouth down on hers.

This time she woke in his arms, feeling warm, safe and sexually sated. If it had been possible to stop time, then she would have picked that moment, because she couldn't imagine ever wanting to be anywhere else.

Watching him sleep, her eyes drifted to the firm contours of his mouth and instantly she felt her body stir. Despite the physical demands of the previous night, she still wanted him.

Again and again—

Perhaps she was more like her mother than she'd thought.

Driven by an impulse that she didn't even try and understand, Lindsay slid a hand over his bare chest, dislodging the sheet so that his body was exposed. Then she pressed her lips against his shoulder blade, slid lower and trailed her mouth over his nipple and down to his hard abdomen. For a moment she lingered in that dangerous, tantalising spot and then she moved lower and found him semi-erect.

Without thinking what she was doing, she took him gently in her mouth and felt him harden instantly. She heard his soft groan and felt the bite of his fingers in her hair as she explored his velvet thickness with her lips and tongue, totally addicted to his body.

The harshness of his breathing told her exactly how he felt about her bold exploration, and then he lifted her and she straddled him, her hair falling forward as she bent to kiss his mouth.

'*Maledizione*—you're incredible,' he groaned and he captured her face in his hands, holding her mouth against his as he kissed her with explicit intent.

Her body was burning and she shifted her pelvis and lowered herself slowly onto his straining shaft, her eyes closing as he filled her. Then his hands dropped to her hips and he held her, guiding her into an erotic rhythm that sent them both rocketing towards another orgasm.

Lindsay flopped onto his chest and he locked his arms around her and kissed the top of her head. His skin was warm against her cheek, the dark hairs of his chest tickling her sensitised flesh.

'*Buon giorno*—good morning.' His voice was huskily amused and his hold on her tightened. 'That was an incredibly good way to be woken up.'

Slightly shocked by how uninhibited she was with him, Lindsay kept her face buried in his neck. She just adored his body and as for what he did to *her* body—

'I could stay on Kingfisher Cay for ever.' *He smells fantastic*, she thought dizzily, pressing her mouth against the bronzed skin of his shoulder.

'You're enjoying the watersports, *tesoro*?' He was still teasing her and this time she lifted her head and looked at him.

'Not just the watersports.' It was her turn to tease. 'Soft sand, turquoise ocean, rainbow fish—'

'And what about the sex?' Supremely confident, he flashed

her a smile that melted the flesh to her bones. 'I thought you didn't want a relationship based on sex—'

Did he know how she felt?

Something shifted inside her, a tiny warning of danger, like a wispy white cloud suddenly appearing in an otherwise perfectly blue sky.

'We don't have a relationship, Alessio,' she breathed, kissing him again before he could say anything else. 'We're just having sex.'

And she wasn't going to think about that now.

Wasn't going to think what the future held for her.

'I can't believe you just said that.' He sank his hands into her tangled blonde hair and kissed her mouth again. 'I could play that back to the television network and make a fortune. Lindsay Lockheart, relationship counsellor, just having sex.'

'I never said that there was anything wrong with sex,' she protested lightly, gasping as his warm skilled hand curved over her bottom. 'Just that it was important not to confuse sex with love and use it as a basis for marriage—Alessio, please— I can't think when you do that—'

'I don't need you to think.' With a powerful movement he rolled her underneath him and looked at her with raw masculine appreciation. 'I've never wanted a woman as much as I want you.'

And that, she thought to herself, her eyes closing as he lowered his head and started to perform yet another miracle on her body, was as big a compliment as any woman was ever likely to hear from the lips of Alessio Capelli.

CHAPTER NINE

'So HAVE you called your sister?' Alessio passed Lindsay a plate of fruit and some tiny pastries.

It was late morning and they were enjoying a leisurely breakfast on the wooden deck that stretched over the water. Exotic fish darted beneath them, sending flashes of dazzling colour through the clear blue water. The only sound was the occasional muted splash as a hummingbird skimmed the water.

'I haven't called her. I haven't switched my phone on since yesterday.' Lindsay hesitated for a moment and then glanced up at him. 'I've done a lot of thinking about what you said. And you were right.'

'About what, exactly?'

Lindsay lowered her gaze and poked at the food on her plate. 'About a lot of things. I *am* too controlling. I've been treating her like a little girl and she isn't a little girl anymore.' She gave a twisted smile. 'To me she's still the vulnerable toddler that used to crawl into bed with me and sleep with her thumb in her mouth. I haven't noticed that she's grown up. Or maybe I did notice and I just didn't want to see it.'

'Stop analysing everything.'

'It's hard not to when you know you've done everything wrong. I've made it difficult for her to turn to me.' She felt a lump in her throat and a sense of helpless frustration because she'd tried so hard to get it right—*to give Ruby the love she hadn't had from their mother.* 'In fact, I've made a real mess of things.'

Alessio didn't respond immediately. When he did, his voice was gruff. 'Lindsay, if this is about what I said to you during the storm—I'm the first to admit that I know nothing about emotions. You shouldn't listen to me. I was probably wrong.'

She couldn't hold back the smile. 'Wrong? You think you might have been wrong? Wow. That's quite an admission coming from you. Shall I tell the press?'

His eyes gleamed. 'You want to tell the press how well you know me?'

Lindsay blushed. 'Maybe not. And anyway, you weren't wrong. You were right about everything you said.' She gave a tiny shrug and a painful smile. 'You were honest. Was that difficult to hear? Yes, it was. But it was also important. You've made me see things more clearly.' She was thinking not only of Ruby, but her mother. 'I need to do things differently. And one of those things is not calling Ruby every five minutes. My hands are itching to pick up that phone and just keep dialling until eventually she picks up, but I know I've got to let go. She'll phone me when she's ready. And when she does, I'll just listen.'

'Why don't you try encouraging your sister and see if that helps?'

'You mean tell her that it's fine to have an affair with Dino? I'm not sure I can go that far—'

'She's having one anyway,' Alessio said dryly, 'with or without your consent. I'm no expert on human behaviour, but it seems to me that the more you try and rein her in, the more she rebels.'

'You're probably right,' Lindsay said humbly. 'I'm just worried about her. Worried that she'll be hurt. I don't want that to happen.'

'Being hurt is part of growing up,' Alessio said unsympathetically. 'She'll be hurt—then she'll toughen up.'

Lindsay hesitated, wondering how much to tell him. 'Not everyone is as strong as you.'

'She won't discover how strong she is with you protecting her all the time. Learning how to get yourself out of the trouble you've created is part of growing up. Why do you feel so responsible for her?'

Lindsay picked at her fruit. 'I'm older than her.' *And she knew what Ruby was capable of doing.*

'And being older than her means that you have to act like her mother?'

'Not just because I'm older.' Lindsay picked up her coffee cup and took a sip, too confused in her head to try and articulate her feelings about her parents. 'Ruby—trusts me. She talks to me. Or she used to. And I've seen her in this situation before. I've seen her so head over heels in love with someone that she can't think straight—that the whole of the rest of her life just seems to go out of the window.'

'That's also part of growing up.'

'Maybe. But last time—' Lindsay broke off, her instinctive discretion warring with a strange desire to confide in him.

Why? Why was she finding it so easy to talk to him? It wasn't as if he were pushing her for information. On the contrary, he was lounging in his chair, totally relaxed, just contributing the odd remark.

The odd, extremely astute remark.

He was a good listener—

'She took pills,' Lindsay said flatly, her hand shaking suddenly as she returned her cup to the saucer. 'Ruby swallowed the contents of a bottle of tablets that a doctor had given her to help her sleep after the break up. And she took them while she was staying in the flat with me. That's how I managed to find her and act so quickly.'

'And you're worried that if it happens again, you won't be around to bail her out.'

'Yes.' It was the intimacy they'd shared, she decided, that made it so easy to talk to him.

'So what are you going to do?' His voice was level. 'Live your life glued to her side so that you can grab her wrist before she opens another bottle?'

Lindsay flinched. 'That's a very lawyer-like response. Hard and factual.'

'Pragmatic,' he drawled softly. 'And you need to stop feeling responsible for her. You can offer support, but you can't live her life. If you try and do that you're just going to be hurt, over and over again.'

'I just hate to see her walking into trouble.'

'How do you know she's in trouble?'

Lindsay glanced at him helplessly. 'Because she didn't turn up to work. Because she's with your brother and it's *obviously* just about sex and—' She broke off, realising that she could just as easily be describing her relationship with Alessio and clearly he was thinking it too because suddenly the tension in the atmosphere snapped tight. 'That sort of relationship is asking for trouble.'

'Is it?' The soft emphasis left her in no doubt that they were no longer talking about Ruby.

The breath caught in her throat. Trouble? *Oh, yes, she was in big trouble* and she knew it. Those ominous clouds that were currently just a shadow on the horizon of her mind would build and build. Sooner or later she was going to have to confront them, but it wasn't going to be now. For now, she was still in the sunshine.

'I'm not the same person as Ruby. I can separate sex from love.' She hoped she sounded convincing, but she was horribly aware of his thoughtful gaze lingering on her face.

Agitated, she stared out across the bay and he watched her

for a long moment and then poured himself another cup of coffee.

'Tell me more about what happened with Ruby the first time.'

'The guy she was seeing—well, he suddenly announced that he was marrying someone else and the end of that relationship was nearly the end of her. Ruby always expects too much of relationships. As soon as a guy looks at her she starts imagining weddings and—' Lindsay broke off and folded her arms around her body, horribly conscious of his penetrative gaze. 'It's my fault. I should have tried harder to persuade her to come back to London.'

Alessio was silent for a moment and then he stirred. 'It sounds as though my brother might have his hands full,' he said dryly, an ironic gleam in his eyes. 'It will do both of them good. And now I don't want to talk about them anymore. I'm tired of my brother and I'm tired of your sister. You've barely eaten anything—are you feeling ill?'

'No.' She flashed him a quick smile and shook her head. 'It's all delicious, I'm just not that hungry.'

'With the amount of physical activity we indulged in last night and this morning,' he drawled softly, 'you should be starving, *tesoro*.'

No one had ever spoken to her in such an intimate way before and she felt herself colour.

'I'm fine. So will you take on the actor as a client?'

'I haven't decided yet.' He stretched his legs out in front of him, staring at the clear ocean.

'Well, he's worth a lot so it would be lucrative.'

'I don't do it for the money.'

'No.' Lindsay spoke quietly. 'I know you don't. You do it for other reasons.'

He turned his head and looked at her, his expression suddenly thoughtful. 'And you think you know those reasons?'

'Well, you obviously don't need the money.' Lindsay

glanced round their island paradise with a faint smile. 'You're a very intelligent man and you obviously find being a lawyer intellectually stimulating. But there's more to it than that, isn't there?'

'Is there?'

'Alessio, you could have chosen to specialise in any number of different areas, but you chose to be a divorce lawyer. And you only act for men. Never women.'

His eyes held hers. 'Clients approach me.'

'But you're very selective about who you act for. Sometimes it seems as though you're trying to get revenge on the whole female sex. And yet I know you don't hate women. I think you just hate women who try and benefit from marriage.' She hesitated. 'Were your parents divorced?' Seeing the sudden tension in his shoulders, she cursed herself softly. 'Sorry,' she muttered. 'None of my business.'

'I come from a tiny village in Sicily, which is still living in another time,' he said evenly. 'Divorce doesn't happen. They handle marital disharmony in an entirely different way.'

'You mean they have affairs.'

'Two people are not meant to be locked together for ever. The best that anyone can hope for is serial monogamy.'

'If your father had lots of affairs, then I can understand why you might come to that conclusion.'

He dragged his gaze from hers and concentrated his attention on a yacht that skimmed past them, the wind inflating the sails. It was a full minute before he responded.

'It wasn't my father who had the affairs,' he said flatly. 'It was my mother. And I can't imagine for a moment why I'm telling you this.'

Lindsay stared at his hard profile, feeling incredibly stupid and exasperated with herself. 'Yes,' she said simply. 'Of course. It would have been your mother.'

'Of course?' He turned then, his eyes glittering dangerously, his face more impossibly handsome than ever. 'Why "of course"?' His tone was brittle and she knew that they'd sailed into dangerous waters, but she still felt warm inside because he *had* confided in her and she knew enough about him to realise the significance of that.

He trusted her.

'How do I know it was your mother? Because you refuse to create an emotional bond with women. Because you rescue men from bad marriages to women who aren't in love with them.'

'You've clearly spent a lot of time analysing me,' he drawled and Lindsay shook her head, sensing his immediate withdrawal.

'Of course I haven't. But we've been together these last few days so it would have been impossible for me to not notice certain things about you—'

'Then you've probably also noticed that I'm not into talking about myself—' he rose to his feet, walked round the table and scooped her into his arms '—and that I have a limitless appetite for sex where you are concerned.'

'Alessio—' Breathless, she wrapped her arms round his neck, but he was already striding back into the bedroom and she gave a low moan as his mouth came down on hers.

Alessio lay staring up at the ceiling, his arms locked around Lindsay's sleeping form. Her body was pressed against his, her head nestled in his shoulder and her silken hair tumbling over his chest.

He hadn't thought about his mother for years—*hadn't allowed himself to go there.*

And before today, he'd never discussed his childhood with another person. He'd never revealed intimate secrets to another person.

And yet, for some reason, he'd told Lindsay Lockheart.

Lindsay, with her deeply ingrained sense of responsibility and her unshakeable belief in the existence of love.

And what had that confession achieved?

It had left him feeling naked and bare, and it had left her feeling as though their relationship had turned a corner.

And it had, he thought grimly. *Just not in the direction she was expecting.*

As far as he was concerned, it was time to make an exit.

His mounting tension must have transmitted itself to her because she stirred, her thigh sliding against his as she shifted slightly in the bed.

Lifting her head, she looked at him, her eyes sleepy. Then she lifted a hand and touched his face. 'I love you,' she murmured and he felt every muscle in his body tense.

'I know you do.'

And he felt a stab of guilt because he knew he should never have let it get this far. A woman like Lindsay, who believed in relationships, who believed in marriage—he should have avoided her like the plague.

'It's late,' he said in a cool tone, extracting himself from the affectionate circle of her arms and springing from the bed like a tiger who had spotted a trap. 'I need to have another meeting with my client. Why don't you have a bath or something? Relax.'

Her blue eyes went from sleepy, to wary, to hurt and she slowly pulled the sheet up over her body, covering herself. 'Fine. I'll do that.'

Her quiet dignity dug into his conscience like a thousand knives and he turned and strolled into his dressing room, anxious to escape. But the guilt followed him and he gritted his teeth and cursed himself for breaking his one unbreakable rule. Never confide in a woman. Never make it personal.

And what had he done?

He'd made it personal.

And now he was paying the price.

* * *

Lindsay slipped into the navy skirt, pulling a face as she zipped it up and realised just how hot and uncomfortable she was going to be in such an unsuitable piece of clothing.

A few days ago this outfit had seemed perfectly comfortable. It had suited the way she felt. The way she approached life.

Now it just felt—well, wrong.

But what choice did she have?

Once again, her tiny overnight bag was in the centre of the floor and when Natalya appeared in the doorway, she looked surprised to find Lindsay packed and ready.

'Oh—I came to tell you that you have an hour to pack because Signor Capelli is flying back to Rome this afternoon. But clearly someone has already given you the message.'

Oh yes, someone had given her the message.

He'd given her the message loud and clear.

And she'd been blaming herself ever since because it was *all* her fault. What had possessed her to think he might like to talk to her about his past? What arrogance had made her think that she could be different?

And what had possessed her to tell him that she loved him?

The moment she'd said those words, Alessio had removed himself from danger faster than a fighter pilot hitting the eject button on a doomed plane.

'Thanks, Natalya.' She managed a smile. 'I'll be at the jetty in an hour.'

An hour.

Alessio Capelli didn't hang around, did he?

But what had she expected?

She'd said, 'I love you.' Half asleep and softened by the intimacies they'd shared, she'd said, 'I love you.' And from that point she'd watched their relationship unravel with super-sonic speed and hideous inevitability, like dropping a ball of wool from the top of the Empire State building.

And that was what happened when you indulged in a wild, crazy affair with no future.

That was what happened when you let physical chemistry dictate choices.

It would have been very easy to wish she hadn't delved into his background, or said those three little words—but she knew that it wouldn't have changed anything. The ending had always been coming.

And she would have done the whole thing again.

She'd made that choice.

Lindsay relaxed in the soft leather seat, pretending to be absorbed in the file on her lap. To add authenticity to the pretence, she occasionally scribbled something in the margin. But she was scribbling nonsense and her mind wasn't on the contents of the file—it was on the man seated opposite her.

Gone was the sexy lover. Alessio Capelli was once more the ruthless divorce lawyer. Since boarding his private jet, he'd been on the telephone, speaking in rapid Italian to a non-stop stream of people who were clearly desperate for his advice.

After one such call he glanced up at her, his handsome face blank of expression. 'There's a message on my phone from Dino. It seems that he and your sister are back in Rome.'

'Oh. Right.'

'He says they're engaged.'

Lindsay wondered why she felt so numb. 'I'm so pleased for them.'

'Pleased?' His dark brows locked in a dangerous frown. 'How can you be pleased? I would have thought it was the last thing you wanted for her.'

'One thing you taught me was that you can't live someone else's life for them,' she murmured, turning her head and looking out of the window. He'd taught her other things too, things she was never going to forget. Like the fact that sometimes the right choice wasn't obvious. 'I hope they'll be happy.'

'They'll probably drive each other up the wall.' He gave a faint smile. 'And I suppose you'll end up counselling them.'

'And if I fail, you'll end up doing their divorce.'

'Stay with me in Rome.' His blunt command was so unexpected that for a moment she simply stared at him.

'Pardon?'

'This doesn't have to be over, Lindsay.'

His words were so unexpected that for a moment she didn't breathe.

He was offering her more.

He wanted to extend their relationship into the future. Sexually, intellectually they would be good together—

Willing to agree to anything that would give them a little more time together, Lindsay opened her mouth to say yes. But she couldn't do it.

How could she say yes, knowing that he didn't feel anything for her? For him, it was all about the sex and she knew that marriages based on sex didn't last.

She wasn't like her mother. For her, the price was too high.

'You're offering me that coveted position as your mistress?' Somehow, she managed to make a joke of it. 'Well, I can certainly see some advantages. For a start I'd be given *that* phone number. At least I'd be able to contact you when I wanted to without having to doorstep you in your office.'

'So is that a yes?'

She blinked several times, frustrated that tears should threaten now. 'No, Alessio, it isn't a yes. How can it be a yes?'

'Because it's what you want.'

'No,' Lindsay said quietly. 'It isn't. I don't want a relationship that's based on sex. This morning I slipped and said "I love you" and that's something that you just don't want to hear.'

'You're probably more comfortable with those words than

I am. I expect you heard "I love you" when you were growing up,' he said gruffly. 'I didn't.'

Lindsay was silent for a moment. 'Let me tell you the truth about my parents' relationship.' She took a deep breath and plunged. 'They weren't happily married at all. In fact, I don't have a single memory that involves them being happy. I didn't hear "I love you". They shared a powerful chemistry and very little else.' She gave a painful smile. 'That chemistry seemed to stop them from acting sensibly. They'd separate and then get back together and then separate again—they couldn't stop having sex, but they couldn't bear each other's company outside the bedroom.' She broke off and glanced at him, but his handsome face was expressionless as he listened.

'Go on.'

She shrugged. 'Even at the age of seven I used to think to myself, "*Why don't the two of you try talking to each other?*" But they just never did. It was hideous. For five minutes it would be delirious happiness because Daddy was home— then they'd vanish to the bedroom and a few hours later the rows would start again.'

'And you witnessed the rows.'

'Rows, sex—my parents didn't seem to think we needed protecting from what was going on. I think they were little more than children themselves.' Lindsay sighed. 'I don't know which was worse—their rows or their divorce. Ruby was the result of one of my parents' many abortive attempts at reconciliation. It didn't work. In fact, having Ruby made things worse. The responsibility of a young baby made it harder for my mother to have a relationship with Dad, so she just abdicated responsibility.'

'So who looked after her?'

Lindsay brushed a speck of dust from her skirt. 'I did.'

Alessio frowned. 'You were seven years old. How could you possibly look after a baby?'

'I'd been looking after myself for several years,' Lindsay told him quietly. 'I just included Ruby in everything I did. I did our washing. I cooked our meals. I hugged her when she cried. Fortunately my school was round the corner so I used to nip home in between lessons and at lunchtime.'

'That explains why you worry about her so much. I often thought you behaved more like a mother than a sister.'

Lindsay rubbed the tips of her fingers over her forehead. 'She actually started to call me Mum when she was about two, but I didn't let her. I wanted her to know that I was her sister, not her Mum. I was too young to understand it all myself, but I think I knew instinctively that she had enough emotional problems without growing up thinking I was her mother.' She looked at him and shrugged. 'It was a mess. I probably didn't handle it right—'

'I think you are incredible,' he said softly and Lindsay faltered, touched by his praise.

'I don't know. Ruby was left very traumatised by the whole thing and I was too young to know how to deal with that. My solution was to smother her in love, but that didn't compensate for the damage done to her confidence and feeling of security. The divorce almost finished her off because Mum blamed her for the whole thing. If she hadn't had Ruby—oh, you can imagine the sort of things she said.'

'I don't think I want to. And what about you, Lindsay? You've talked a lot about your sister and the effect it had on her.' His voice was low. 'What about the effect it had on you?'

For a moment she didn't answer. Then she stirred. 'Well, it made me interested in psychology. And it has taught me that passion isn't a good basis for a marriage. But you already know that. You see that every day in your work.'

'So you want a marriage without passion?' His incredulous tone made her laugh.

'No. No, I don't want that. I'm far too greedy to settle for that.' She met his gaze. 'Which is why I'm turning down your invitation. But thank you.' She smiled. 'Thank you for asking.'

'Greedy? What is it that you want?'

'Oh—' she leaned her head back against her seat, her expression wistful '—the whole dream. I want the passion, yes. But I also want a man who excites me in other ways—a man who is going to love me for who I am, who'll stick with me when things get difficult and who will genuinely care about me.' She glanced at him and shrugged, trying to laugh at herself. 'And that, I suppose, is why I'm still single and likely to stay that way.'

'Lindsay—'

She held up a hand because the whole thing was hard enough without him trying to persuade her. 'Don't say anything else. I don't regret what happened between us, if that's what you want to know. In the end you won, Alessio. I couldn't resist you. But I'd do the whole thing again in a moment. You've changed the way I look at the past—made me understand things about myself that I didn't really understand before.' She frowned. 'I can't forgive Mum for the way she treated Ruby, but at least now I understand a little bit more about how passion can take over.' She blinked several times. 'I can see the runway lights. We're about to land.'

It was over.

CHAPTER TEN

Two weeks later, driven to the point of combustion by yet another wealthy, demanding client, Alessio strode out of the glass meeting room towards the lift.

What the hell was the matter with him?

He used to relish the mental stimulation of his job, but since his return from the Caribbean it had been nothing but a source of irritation.

His mobile phone buzzed and he lunged into his pocket and retrieved it, swiftly scanning the caller's number. Realising that the call was from a Russian supermodel he'd been dating a few months earlier, he gritted his teeth, rejected the call and dropped the phone back in his pocket, appalled by the depth of his own disappointment.

What had he expected?

Lindsay Lockheart telling him she'd changed her mind about having an affair with him?

She didn't want that, did she?

Clearly she wasn't feeling anywhere near the depth of frustration that *he* was.

Loosening his tie with an impatient yank of his fingers, Alessio scowled as one of his team called his name and hurried up behind him.

Now what?

Hadn't he made it clear that he wanted to be on his own?

Visibly nervous, the man stepped into the lift with him. 'I assume from the questions you asked, that you're not prepared to take the case?'

'What case?' His mind still on Lindsay Lockheart, Alessio snapped out the words and his junior colleague blinked in confusion, glancing back towards the meeting room as if checking there hadn't been some mistake.

'Well—*that* case,' he muttered awkwardly. 'He was hoping you'd take it on—at the moment his wife is so angry about his affair that she's threatening to take him to the cleaners.'

'Good for her.'

'I beg your pardon?' Unable to hide his astonishment, his colleague fumbled with the file in his hands. 'You—I don't—he wants your advice.'

'Enrico,' Alessio's voice was cool. 'How old are those children?'

Clearly startled by the question, the man checked the file. 'The older girl is eight, the other one is a baby. Two little girls.'

Two little girls. Two little girls, whose lives were being smashed to pieces.

His mind on Lindsay Lockheart, Alessio took a deep breath.

'She deserves every penny she can get. And my advice is that he should start thinking about his children and his responsibilities, instead of his own investments.'

Gaping at him, his junior colleague ran a finger around his collar as if it were strangling him. 'So you want me to tell him—what exactly?'

Alessio couldn't dispel the image of wide blue eyes and soft blonde hair.

'Tell him to try couples counselling.' His tone biting and sharp, he strode out of the lift and into his office, his body aching so badly it was almost a physical pain.

His personal assistant was hovering, looking harassed. 'Your three o'clock meeting has been rescheduled.'

'Why?'

'Because there are too many journalists outside the building. You don't want to go out there right now—it's being dealt with.'

With an impatient frown, Alessio strode across to the window and stared down at the street below. Even from this height he could see the pack of photographers surrounding the front door of the Capelli offices.

'For the past two weeks I've lived the life of a monk,' he breathed. 'What exactly are they after this time?'

'Nothing new. Still the Lindsay Lockheart thing.' His assistant put a neat pile of papers on his desk. 'You asked for these—'

'*What* Lindsay Lockheart thing?'

'She's been in the papers every day for the past two weeks.'

There was a brief, deadly silence while Alessio digested that information. 'And you didn't think it worth mentioning?' His tone silky soft, he watched as the woman paled.

'You're not normally interested in what the tabloids have to say about your love life—'

'You have precisely two minutes in which to produce a copy of every paper that has mentioned Lindsay Lockheart's name in the last two weeks. You then have a further minute to get the head of PR into my office.' Struggling to contain the volcanic eruption of his temper, Alessio strode to his desk and punched the number of Lindsay's flat into his phone. Her ansaphone clicked on and he cut the connection angrily just as his secretary returned with the papers.

Was she screening calls?

He scanned each paper in grim silence, his temper rising with each line of newsprint he read. Then dropped them onto his desk and strode towards the door.

* * *

Why couldn't they leave her alone?

Lindsay slammed the pillow over her head to shut out the insistent noise of the buzzer. Ever since she'd returned from the Caribbean, she'd had photographers camped on her doorstep. Trapped in her flat, she'd been unable to leave even to buy milk, but it didn't matter because she couldn't face food. She couldn't summon the energy to move.

Every now and then her ansaphone clicked and her heart raced because she couldn't stop hoping that it was *him*. But it never was. Every time the phone rang it was just another client cancelling an appointment.

Her business was ruined. Everything she was—everything she believed—had collapsed around her. It should have been a terrible blow but the awful thing was she didn't even care.

It seemed that *nothing* hurt as much as the fact that Alessio hadn't called.

Sooner or later she was going to have to pull herself together and work out what she was going to do with the rest of her life, but for now she didn't have the energy to move.

And there was no point in moving because her every action was caught on camera for the public to see and comment on.

But could it be any worse?

Did she really care if they took pictures of her without make-up, in rumpled clothes? Could they hurt her any more than they already had?

The thing that had upset her most had been the photographs taken on Kingfisher Cay. *Someone* had snapped them having dinner and the accompanying stories were all about the fact that she'd spent a whole night in his villa. And the stories were sensationalist and tasteless, embellished to sell more copies to a public always hungry for mindless gossip and the humiliation of others.

They'd made her relationship with Alessio sound like some seedy little fling.

And it hadn't been like that.

And it hurt really, really badly. But nowhere near as much as the fact that Alessio hadn't called.

On the plus side, she'd spoken to Ruby, who was very happy and living in Rome with Dino Capelli. And somehow her happiness made Lindsay feel even worse. She'd been so sure about her choices, but now—

Now she wasn't sure about anything.

With a sniff, she pulled the duvet over her head to block out the sound of the buzzer.

Why didn't they go away and leave her alone?

Guilt permeating every fibre of his being, Alessio elbowed his way through the banks of paparazzi crowding outside Lindsay's flat.

'Hey, Alessio—have you come back for seconds?'

With a low growl, Alessio picked the photographer up by his collar and backed him against the wall. 'Clear off,' he muttered thickly, 'and do something about your own life instead of prying into other people's.'

Flashes erupted around him and he knew that he'd just given the press still more fodder for the next day's salacious headlines.

'You'd better watch that temper of yours, Alessio,' the man spluttered and Alessio gave a slow, dangerous smile.

'I'm completely in control.' He didn't slacken his grip. 'Trust me, when I lose my temper, you'll be the first to know.'

'This is assault—'

'No—' Alessio's voice was icy cold as he released the man '—what *you* do is assault. Remember that, because you're starting to annoy me.' His handsome face a mask of disdain, he flicked some dirt from the sleeve of his perfectly cut designer suit. 'And I'm not at my best when I'm annoyed.'

'You can't threaten me.' Blustering and glancing towards

his colleagues for support, the photographer cast a wary glance at the hard set of Alessio's features. 'You can't touch me.'

Alessio's mouth curved into a smile. 'No?'

'I suppose you think I should be scared because you're some hotshot lawyer.' The man was sweating now and Alessio studied him with cool contempt.

'No,' he said softly, 'not because of that.' He reached forward and straightened the man's collar carefully. 'Because I'm Sicilian.'

The man swallowed. 'Are you threatening me?'

Alessio smiled. 'Certainly not.' His eyes lingered on the man's face until the photographer paled and started to shift uncomfortably.

'That's coercion,' he muttered and Alessio lifted an eyebrow. 'What is?'

The man backed off. 'If you ask me that girl's crazy to have anything to do with you. You're bloody lethal.' But the pack of paparazzi all withdrew slightly as Alessio slowly reached into the inside pocket of his suit.

'You want a story?' Laughing at their complete lack of spine, Alessio withdrew a piece of paper and toyed with it for a moment. 'This story should give you a comfortable retirement.' And with that he flicked the paper carelessly towards the banks of photographers, smiling at the resulting mayhem.

Let them take pieces out of each other. He had better things to do.

Turning his back on them, he took the steps to the front door two at a time and buzzed Lindsay's flat.

The crash of her front door opening roused her from her inertia and Lindsay sat upright in bed, clutching the duvet to her chest, frozen in horror.

They'd broken her door down—

Fumbling for her phone, she was about to call the police

when Alessio strode into her bedroom, his eyes glinting dark as anthracite, his mouth a grim line.

Her first emotion was one of unutterable joy.

And then she realised that he wasn't here because of her. He was here because of *him*. Because of the newspapers.

It only took a glance for her to realise that he was positively vibrating with anger.

'Y-you broke my door down.' He looked so impossibly handsome that it was all she could do not to fling her arms round him.

'What was I supposed to do? You didn't answer the doorbell.' He made it sound like a perfectly logical action given the circumstances, and for the first time in days she almost laughed.

'I didn't answer the door because I didn't want to see anyone. And you've let the press in—'

'There are eight security guards planted outside your door,' he growled. 'The press won't be bothering you again.'

Lindsay gave a strangled laugh. 'Eight? You don't think that's overkill?'

'No, I do not. And you should have more concern for your own privacy.'

'What was I supposed to do? I'm not a billionaire, Alessio. I'm just—me.'

The phone rang again and she tensed, bracing herself for the usual. The ansaphone clicked on and yet another client left a message cancelling their next appointment. Wishing he hadn't witnessed that, Lindsay gave a fatalistic smile. 'You see? I can't afford security guards even if I wanted them. I no longer have a job.'

He was glaring at the ansaphone as if it had slighted him personally. 'Your clients are cancelling?'

'Yes.' What was the point of lying? Lindsay shrugged. 'It seems you're not the only one who thinks I'm not qualified to advise anyone on how to maintain a relationship. I suppose you've come so that you can say "I told you so" in person.'

'*Why* are they cancelling?'

'I suppose they no longer trust my judgment,' Lindsay mumbled, suddenly weary. *What was he doing here?* 'And I can hardly blame them for that. It's fine, Alessio. I'm fine. Just go. Savour your victory.'

'I'm *not* leaving.' He strode across to her window and closed the blinds.

'What are you doing?'

'Reducing the opportunities for the pack of wolves outside to take photographs. You really need to learn to protect yourself—you're *shockingly* naïve.'

She blinked. 'This is a fourth-floor flat, Alessio. You think they're going to climb up the drainpipe?'

'Have you noticed the scaffolding being erected opposite?'

'I haven't looked out of the window for two days—' Realising what she'd just admitted, Lindsay looked away. 'It's been a bit—difficult.'

'You've let the press trap you in your flat?'

'Well, yes, I suppose I have.'

'*Maledizione*, why didn't you call me?'

'Because that number you gave me is reserved for your lovers, and I'm not your lover anymore.' Her voice was croaky and black, stormy eyes connected with hers.

'You should have called—*I had no idea*—'

'You have an entire press department—'

'A press department who know I don't usually waste my time reading the sort of trash written by those sharks outside your door!'

Lindsay swallowed. *He hadn't known?* 'Right. So you're telling me—'

'I'm telling you that I found out what was happening less than four hours ago.'

'And if you'd known?'

'Well, for a start you wouldn't have been trapped in your flat for two weeks. But we can rectify that.' Removing his phone, he made one brief call, speaking in low, rapid Italian. Then he pulled open the door of her wardrobe, pulled out a pair of trousers and a shirt and flung it on the bed. 'Get dressed.'

'Why?'

Prowling round her bedroom, he found her shoes. 'Call me fussy, but I don't want naked pictures of my future wife plastered all over the newspapers.'

'Your—' Lindsay gaped at him. 'What did you just say?'

Vibrating with tension, Alessio paced across her bedroom and grabbed her handbag. 'You're going to marry me. Is your passport in here?'

'Alessio—'

'We'll leave everything else here.' He glanced around her flat impatiently. 'We can clear it out another time. Are you going to get dressed?'

'Alessio, you just said—' She broke off as her phone rang again and yet another client called to cancel.

Swearing first in Italian and then in English, Alessio yanked the phone cable out of the wall. 'I've had enough of hearing that. They are all idiots—' He gave up on English and let out a stream of Italian, none of which she understood.

'Alessio!' Lindsay slid out of the bed. 'Stop ranting and raving and *talk* to me for a minute! You're not making any sense.'

'I'm making perfect sense. Is your passport in your handbag?'

'Yes, but—Alessio, you just said you were going to marry me!'

'I *am* going to marry you. But first I want to get you back to Rome.' His tone raw, he sank his long fingers into his glossy dark hair in a gesture of frustration. 'I can't protect you here.'

Her legs failing to hold her, Lindsay plopped back onto the bed. 'You can't be serious—'

'It's just too exposed. I own a villa outside Rome. I'm taking you there.'

'No, I mean—about marrying me.' She gave a disbelieving laugh and tried to sort out her muddled head. 'What is this? A sudden rush of chivalry? You think because our affair is all over the newspapers, you have to marry me?'

'It has nothing to do with the newspapers.' He crossed the room and hauled her to her feet again. 'You're going to marry me because I want you with me. Always.'

'Alessio—'

'Have you any idea what the last two weeks have been like for me?'

'I thought you said you hadn't seen the newspapers—'

'I'm not talking about the newspapers.' He cupped her face in his hands, his eyes fierce as he looked down at her. 'I'm talking about just not being with you. I—missed you.'

The words were so unexpected that for a moment she didn't reply. 'You missed me in your bed.'

'Well, yes, obviously—' he gave a brief frown '—but not just that. I missed having you around. I like what you have to say—'

'You disagree with me—'

'Invariably—' his eyes gleamed with sardonic humour '—but *always* I find you interesting.'

'You do? You find me interesting?' Her heart was thudding hard against her chest and he gave a groan and lowered his mouth to hers.

'Yes. You're the only woman who has ever been truly honest with me and the sex is amazing. I've missed doing this.' He kissed her slowly and surely and Lindsay sagged against him, her head spinning and her heart so full she felt as though it might burst through her chest.

'You've missed the sex.' She muttered the words against his mouth and he lifted his head and gave a slow, dangerous smile.

'Of course.' And then the smile faded and he stroked her cheeks with his thumbs. 'But most of all I missed *you*. I missed the way you talk and the way you listen. I missed your honesty and your sweetness.'

'Alessio—'

'I want you with me permanently.'

Everything inside her softened and emotion rushed through her. 'You're blaming yourself—'

'*Sì*, I am. This whole situation is *my* fault. But I'll make it up to you.'

She reminded herself that it was just his guilty conscience talking. 'Alessio, I don't want to build my business again. What do I know about relationships? Nothing. I was so convinced that if I could just help people talk to each other, they could sort things out. But all I was really doing was trying to compensate for not being able to sort my parents' marriage out.' Having admitted that, she pulled away from him, finding the whole thing really difficult. 'The truth is that relationships come in all shapes and sizes, and what works for some won't work for others. And sometimes passion on its own can be enough. Marriage isn't everything.'

'You don't believe that.' Alessio picked up the clothes and stuffed them into her hands. 'If you're not dressed in the next two minutes then I'll dress you myself.'

Wondering what had got into him, Lindsay pulled on her trousers, fastened her shirt and pinned her hair into a neat coil. 'There. Satisfied?'

'I won't be satisfied until you're wearing my ring every day and lying in my bed every night,' Alessio breathed and her heart skipped a beat as she looked into his eyes.

'That's a pretty big gesture,' she said shakily, 'even for a guy with a guilty conscience.'

'It isn't a gesture.'

'Oh, Alessio, this isn't fair.' She covered her face with her hands. 'Please, for once, see it from my point of view. This gorgeous, sexy guy who I— This gorgeous sexy guy offers me marriage, but I know it's never going to work so I have to turn him down.'

'Why would you turn me down?'

Her hands dropped to her sides and she looked at him with frustration, breaking up inside because he'd offered her what she wanted, knowing that she'd never take it. 'Because guilt isn't a good basis for a long-term relationship. And it's cruel of you, Alessio—' Her voice broke. 'It's cruel of you to stand there saying these things when you know I have to refuse.'

His eyes glittered hard. 'I'm not letting you refuse. Why would I let you refuse when I know you're desperate to be with me?'

She caught her breath. 'Well, it's nice to know your ego hasn't suffered a blow.'

He swore under his breath. 'We've always been honest with each other, but you're not being honest with me now.'

'Of course I am.'

Alessio raised an eyebrow. 'So finish your sentence, *tesoro*. What was it you said? This gorgeous, sexy guy who I—who you what?'

Lindsay swallowed and looked away. 'Just go away, Alessio,' she muttered. 'On balance it's easier to deal with the paparazzi than you.'

'You were going to say, *this gorgeous, sexy guy who I love*.' His tone soft, he pulled her back into his arms. 'I *know* you love me, Lindsay. You told me.'

'And you ran away so fast you almost tripped.'

'Running away was a reflex action. A lot of women have

used those words and you have to understand that it's instinctive for me to back off.' He gave a driven sigh. 'And it's true that it took me a while to get used to the idea that you love me. But I have done that, and it's fine.'

Lindsay gaped at him in disbelief. 'What?' She gave a tiny laugh. 'You're saying that it's OK for me to love you? That you're going to *let* me? You're so arrogant, Alessio!'

'No, I'm not saying that. Let me finish.' He ran a hand over the back of his neck. 'This is so hard.'

'It isn't hard, Alessio.' She looked at him wearily, all the fight draining out of her. 'I fell in love with you, yes. But as you rightly point out, I'm not the first woman to do that. You've walked away before, you can walk away again. And you don't need to feel guilty about any of this.' She waved a hand vaguely towards the window. 'I honestly don't care. They've probably done me a favour. I needed a change.'

'How much of a change?' His voice hoarse, he took her face in his hands again, tilting her chin so that she was forced to look at him. 'Would it be too much of a change to be married to a wicked Sicilian divorce lawyer?'

'You don't believe in marriage, Alessio.'

'I think expecting two people to stay together is asking a lot,' he admitted, 'unless they truly love each other.'

She stilled. 'What you feel is passion. And passion is no better a basis for a marriage than guilt.'

'That's true, and I understand *why* you believe that after what you told me about your parents. But you're missing one important fact and that's that you can have passion *and* love,' he murmured, taking her face in his hands. 'And that's what we have.'

'No, we don't.'

'I know I'm not saying the right things, but I'm not good at this! I've never told a woman that I love her, before! I'm probably saying it all wrong.'

Lindsay stilled. 'You haven't said it at all.'

'*Sì*, I told you.' His tone was impatient. 'I told you that I love you.'

'No.' She covered her mouth with her hand and shook her head. 'No, you didn't say that to me.' Her legs turned to jelly.

'Well, I'm saying it now,' he growled, removing her hand so that he could crush his mouth against hers. 'I love you, *tesoro*.'

She felt light-headed and terrified at the same time. Terrified of believing him. 'You've never loved anyone—'

'No.' He folded her in his arms. 'I haven't. I saw how much pain loving my mother caused my father. In the small village in Sicily where I grew up, divorce just wasn't an option. And frankly, I don't know whether he would have divorced her even if he'd been given the chance. But I lived with his misery and I felt—helpless. I suppose that's why I saw divorce as a good thing. He should have moved on—maybe met someone else.'

Lindsay looked up at him, understanding. 'It's so hard when you're a child—you want to help, and you can't. And they think it's just about them, but it affects you, too.'

Alessio nodded. 'I've never talked to anyone about it before.'

'You don't have to tell me—'

'I want to. You need to know what you're marrying.' His gaze was wary. 'I'm not exactly experienced when it comes to relationships, but I know you are so I'm relying on you to teach me what I need to know.'

Lindsay gazed at him, tears blurring her vision. 'You really think you love me?'

'I *know* I love you.' He gave a wry smile. 'And if you knew how much I'd changed over the past two weeks, you wouldn't even question me. Twice I've suggested to prospective clients that they try counselling and just this morning—' He broke off and Lindsay looked at him quizzically.

'What happened this morning?'

Alessio's face hardened. 'He had two little girls,' he muttered, 'and I couldn't stop thinking of you and Ruby.'

'You didn't take the case?'

He hesitated. 'We're going to act for the wife.'

Lindsay gave a soft gasp and then laughed. 'You're kidding?'

'I want to make sure those two little girls suffer as little as possible. You see what you've done to me?' A gleam in his eyes, Alessio dragged her back into his arms. 'I'm going to be a magnet for every gold-digger in the Western hemisphere.'

'Just as long as they're only interested in your professional skills,' Lindsay murmured, standing on tiptoe and pressing her mouth against his. 'I'm proud of you. And I *do* love you. Very, very much.'

'Just keep saying it.' Alessio hugged her tightly. 'And now I need to give the press something to photograph.' He took her left hand and slipped an enormous diamond solitaire onto her finger.

'Oh, Alessio—' tears blurred her vision '—it's beautiful.' But the most beautiful thing was the fact that he loved her. 'I can't believe this is happening.'

'Well, it is. And now stop crying or the press will think I've been doing unspeakable things to you. Are you ready to face the world?'

Still staring at the ring, Lindsay gave a weak laugh. 'Every woman with a pulse is going to want to know how I persuaded you to marry me.'

'Well, they're just going to have to work it out for themselves,' Alessio drawled, leading her towards the door. 'From now on I'm not sharing you with anyone.'

As they walked out onto the pavement flashbulbs exploded in their faces and a voice called out, 'Hey, Lindsay, you're wearing a ring! Care to tell everyone your secret?'

Turning to face the bank of cameras, Lindsay smiled. She couldn't *stop* smiling. 'You'd better listen carefully because this is the last piece of relationship advice I'm ever going to give.' Almost bursting with happiness, she clutched Alessio's hand and smiled up at him, her eyes misting. But when she spoke, the words were intended for him. 'The secret,' she said softly, 'was love.'

* * * * *

Celebrate 60 years of pure reading pleasure
with Harlequin®!

Harlequin Presents® is proud to introduce i
ts gripping new miniseries,
THE ROYAL HOUSE OF KAREDES.
An exquisite coronation diamond, split as a symbol of a
warring royal family's feud, is missing! But whoever
reunites the diamond halves will rule all....

Welcome to eight brand-new titles that unfold to reveal the
stories of kings and queens, princes and princesses torn
apart by pride and power, but finally reunited by love.

Step into the world of Karedes with
BILLIONAIRE PRINCE, PREGNANT MISTRESS
Available July 2009
from Harlequin Presents®.

ALEXANDROS KAREDES, SNOW DUSTING the shoulders of his leather jacket and glittering like jewels in his dark hair, stood at the door. Maria felt the blood drain from her head.

"Good evening, Ms. Santos."

His voice was as she remembered it. Deep. Husky. Perfect English, but with the faintest hint of a Greek accent. And cold, as cold as it had been that awful morning she would never forget, when he'd accused her of horrible things, called her terrible names....

"Aren't you going to ask me in?"

She fought for composure. Last time they'd faced each other, they'd been on his turf. Now they were on hers. She was in command here, and that meant everything.

"There's a sign on the door downstairs," she said, her tone every bit as frigid as his. "It says, 'No soliciting or vagrants.'"

His lips drew back in a wolfish grin. "Very amusing."

"What do you want, Prince Alexandros?"

A tight smile eased across his mouth and it killed her that even now, knowing he was a vicious, arrogant man, she couldn't help but notice what a handsome mouth it was. Chiseled. Generous. Beautiful, like the rest of him, which made him living proof that beauty could, indeed, be only skin deep.

"Such formality, Maria. You were hardly so proper the last time we were together."

She knew his choice of words was deliberate. She felt her face heat; she couldn't help that but she damned well didn't have to let him lure her into a verbal sparring match.

"I'll ask you once more, your highness. What do you want?"

"Ask me in and I'll tell you."

"I have no intention of asking you in. Tell me why you're here or don't. It's your choice, just as it will be my choice to shut the door in your face."

He laughed. It infuriated her but she could hardly blame him. He was tall—six two, six three—and though he stood with one shoulder leaning against the door frame, hands tucked casually into the pockets of the jacket, his pose was deceptive. He was strong, with the leanly muscled body of a well-trained athlete.

She remembered his body with painful clarity. The feel of him under her hands. The power of him moving over her. The taste of him on her tongue.

Suddenly, he straightened, his laughter gone. "I have not come this distance to stand in your doorway," he said coldly, "and I am not going to leave until I am ready to do so. I suggest you stand aside and stop behaving like a petulant child."

A petulant child? Was that what he thought? This man who had spent hours making love to her and had then accused her of—of trading her body for profit?

Except it had not been love, it had been sex. And the sooner she got rid of him, the better.

She let go of the doorknob and stepped aside. "You have five minutes."

He strolled past her, bringing cold air and the scent of the night with him. She swung toward him, arms folded. He reached past her, pushed the door closed, then folded his arms, too. She wanted to open the door again but she'd be damned if she was going to get into a who's-in-charge-here argument with him. She was in charge, and he would surely see a tussle over the ground rules as a sign of weakness.

Instead, she looked past him at the big clock above her work table.

"Ten seconds gone," she said briskly. "You're wasting time, your highness."

"What I have to say will take longer than five minutes."

"Then you'll just have to learn to economize. More than five minutes, I'll call the police."

Instantly, his hand was wrapped around her wrist. He tugged her toward him, his dark-chocolate eyes almost black with anger.

"You do that and I'll tell every tabloid shark I can contact about how Maria Santos tried to buy a five-hundred-thousand-dollar commission by seducing a prince." He smiled thinly. "They'll lap it up."

* * * * *

What will it take for this billionaire prince to realize he's falling in love with his mistress...?
Look for
BILLIONAIRE PRINCE, PREGNANT MISTRESS
by Sandra Marton
Available July 2009 from Harlequin Presents®.

We'll be spotlighting a different series every month
throughout 2009 to celebrate our 60th anniversary.

Look for Harlequin® Presents in July!

TWO CROWNS, TWO ISLANDS, ONE LEGACY

A royal family, torn apart by pride and its lust for
power, reunited by purity and passion

Step into the world of Karedes
beginning this July with

BILLIONAIRE PRINCE, PREGNANT MISTRESS
by
Sandra Marton

Eight volumes to collect and treasure!

HARLEQUIN *Presents*

EXTRA

FORCED TO MARRY

Wives for the taking!

Once these men put a diamond ring on their bride's finger, there's no going back....

Wedlocked and willful, these wives will get a wedding night they'll never forget!

Read all the fantastic stories, out this month in Harlequin Presents EXTRA:

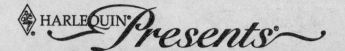

HARLEQUIN *Presents*

International Billionaires

Life is a game of power and pleasure.
And these men play to win!

THE SHEIKH'S LOVE-CHILD
by *Kate Hewitt*

When Lucy arrives in the desert kingdom of Biryal,
Sheikh Khaled's eyes are blacker and harder than
before. But Lucy and the sheikh are inextricably
bound forever—for he is the father of her son....

Book #2838

Available July 2009

Two more titles to collect in this exciting miniseries:
BLACKMAILED INTO THE GREEK
TYCOON'S BED by *Carol Marinelli*
August

THE VIRGIN SECRETARY'S
IMPOSSIBLE BOSS by *Carole Mortimer*
September

TWO CROWNS, TWO ISLANDS, ONE LEGACY

A royal family, torn apart by pride and its lust for power, reunited by purity and passion

coming in 2009

8 volumes to collect and treasure!

REQUEST YOUR FREE BOOKS!